"I hope that whatever you're staring at is worth staying after school."

"Excuse me," Lucas drawled, his deep voice loud in the quiet room. "I wonder if you could help me?"

The unfamiliar adult male voice wasn't the teenage tenor that Jennifer had been expecting. The sidelong glimpse she'd caught of a tall, jeans-clad form at the hall door had led her to believe that one of her students had been staring at her.

She looked over her shoulder, her gaze widening as she took in the cowboy in her doorway. His tall, broad body nearly filled the opening. Beneath his black Stetson, deep blue eyes watched her with unreadable intensity. Jennifer felt the tiny hairs on the back of her neck rise, and every survival instinct she owned went on instant alert.

This man wasn't one of the mild-mannered, easily discouraged males she cultivated as friends. This man was *trouble*.

Dear Reader,

It wouldn't be summer without romance, or June without a wedding—and Special Edition brings you both this month!

Our very romantic THAT'S MY BABY! title for June is *Happy Father's Day,* by Barbara Faith. In fact, this daddy has *six* adopted children he calls his own! Now he has to convince the woman of his dreams to become part of his family.

What would June be without blushing brides? Well, first we have book two of Christine Flynn's miniseries, THE WHITAKER BRIDES. In *The Rebel's Bride,* it's renegade Caleb Whitaker's turn to walk down the aisle. And *Waiting at the Altar* is where you'll find ever-faithful Jacob Matthews—this time, he's determined to be a groom at last in book two of Amy Frazier's series, SWEET HOPE WEDDINGS. In Gail Link's *Marriage-To-Be?* the nuptials are still in question—it's up to the bride to choose between two brothers.

Rounding out the month are two authors new to Special Edition. Janis Reams Hudson has a sexy tale in store when two sparring lovers issue the challenge, *Resist Me if You Can.* And after Lois Faye Dyer's *Lonesome Cowboy* meets his match in a spirited schoolteacher, his lonely days just might be over.

So don't miss a moment of these wonderful books. It's just the beginning of a summer filled with love and romance from Special Edition!

Sincerely,

Tara Gavin,
Senior Editor

Please address questions and book requests to:
Silhouette Reader Service
U.S.: 3010 Walden Ave., P.O. Box 1325, Buffalo, NY 14269
Canadian: P.O. Box 609, Fort Erie, Ont. L2A 5X3

LOIS FAYE DYER

LONESOME COWBOY

SPECIAL EDITION®

Published by Silhouette Books
America's Publisher of Contemporary Romance

For my mother-in-law, Anita, with love and affection. Never-failing good cheer and smiles like yours are hard to find.

 SILHOUETTE BOOKS

ISBN 0-373-24038-4

LONESOME COWBOY

Copyright © 1996 by Lois Faye Dyer

This edition published by arrangement with Harlequin Books S.A.

® and TM are trademarks of Harlequin Books S.A., used under license. Trademarks indicated with ® are registered in the United States Patent and Trademark Office, the Canadian Trade Marks Office and in other countries.

Printed in U.S.A.

LOIS FAYE DYER,

winner of the 1989-1990 _Romantic Times_ Reviewer's Choice Award for Best New Series Author, lives on Washington State's beautiful Puget Sound with her husband and their yellow Lab, Maggie Mae. She ended a career as a paralegal and Superior Court clerk to fulfill a lifelong dream to write. When she's not involved in writing, she enjoys long walks on the beach with her husband, watching musical and Western movies from the 1940s and 1950s, and, most of all, indulging her passionate addiction to reading. This is her sixth published novel.

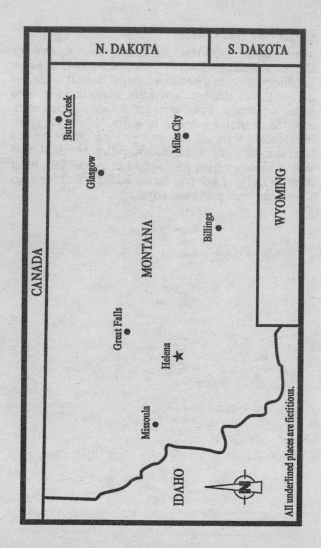

N. DAKOTA

S. DAKOTA

CANADA

Butte Creek

Glasgow

Miles City

Billings

MONTANA

WYOMING

Great Falls

Helena

Missoula

IDAHO

N

All underlined places are fictitious.

Chapter One

Lucas Hightower swore with irritation and shot a blue-eyed glare at his watch. The scratched, silver-trimmed face with its worn black leather band was sturdy, plain and serviceable, and it told him that he was going to be late for his appointment with Annabel Fitch.

I wonder why she wants to see me? he thought, lifting his battered Stetson to wipe the moisture from his forehead with the back of his wrist. *And why she didn't just ask me on the phone?*

Lucas tugged the Stetson's brim lower over his forehead and stared consideringly off across the pasture. It was only mid-May, but the afternoon sun beat relentlessly down from the inverted blue bowl of Montana sky. As always, surveying the rolling acres of the Lazy H filled Lucas with a deep sense of peace and fierce pride.

"Oh, hell," he muttered with a resigned shrug of broad shoulders. Annabel Fitch was his old high school English teacher and one of the few women he genuinely liked and respected. If she wanted to speak to him in her office, he'd be there. It was the least he could do.

He threw the posthole digger and shovel into the bed of the dusty pickup and yanked open the cab door to climb inside. A pair of wire cutters, forgotten in the back pocket of his faded jeans, jabbed him and he grunted, yanking them out and tossing them onto the seat beside him. Then he pushed in the clutch and turned the ignition key. The powerful engine turned over with a muted roar and he shifted into first gear to ease the truck over the rough dips and bumps of the pasture.

"Hey, Josh," he called, braking to a stop beside his brother, who was working his way up the line of fence posts. "I'm going into town—do you need anything?"

Josh Hightower gave a final stamp to the loose dirt at the base of a peeled-pole fence post and turned to look at him.

"Yeah." Beneath the brim of a disreputable-looking, battered cowboy hat, Josh's blue-green eyes were faintly bloodshot and underlined with dark shadows. Black stubble shadowed his jaw. "About a quart of aspirin."

"Too much whiskey and poker last night?" Lucas's eyes narrowed and darkened, his face going cold and still.

"My head feels too big to get through a doorway today—and I lost fifty dollars to Doc Hansen. You should have been there, maybe he would have taken some of your money and I wouldn't have lost as much."

"In that case, I'm glad I spent most of the night in the barn with Maggie."

"Lucas." Josh's hard expression turned cynical and he shook his head. "You've got to get a life. There's something wrong with a man who'd rather spend the night with a mare than playing poker and drinking good whiskey."

Lucas shook his head, his voice hard. "There's no such thing as good whiskey."

"You may have a point there," Josh agreed with a shrug.

Lucas let out the clutch and the truck began to roll slowly forward. "I'll be back before supper," he said. "If you finish this string of fence, the north pasture has loose wire and posts about a mile from the gate on Colby's side."

"Right." Josh didn't argue with Lucas's orders. The Lazy H was his brother's life and blood. It was no mystery that Lucas hadn't married; the ranch had been his mistress for more than half of his thirty-three years.

As Lucas drove off, he fought a wave of worry over his brother. The concern was becoming an all-too-frequent companion.

It's been more than two months since Sarah Drummond left town, he thought with irritation. *When is he going to get over her?* Lucas hated feeling helpless, and the truth was, there was little he could do to ease his brother's grieving over Sarah. Josh refused to discuss what had happened. All Lucas knew for sure was that Josh was suffering—and that he was drinking and fighting with nearly anyone who so much as spoke to him.

The truck lurched to the right and Lucas turned his wandering attention back to the wheel as the pickup bumped and rolled over the rough ground. He had less than half an hour to make the thirty-mile drive to Butte Creek.

The chalk moved smoothly across the surface of the blackboard, completing the first quote from Shakespeare's *Macbeth* in graceful, curving, white-against-black script. Jennifer McCleary stopped writing and checked her watch for the fifth time in as many minutes.

He's late. Maybe he isn't coming. She frowned, the graceful wings of her pale brown eyebrows veeing downward above gold eyes, where irritation mixed with concern. Her chin firmed with resolve. Mrs. Fitch's plan to enlist Lucas Hightower's help with Trey Webber was the best solution they could conceive for the troubled teenager. She was determined that the rancher was going to cooperate. *But first we have to convince him, and we can't do that unless we can talk to him.*

She stared at the blackboard, but instead of seeing the lines from Shakespeare, she was remembering her meeting with the principal only two days before.

The coach had found a bottle of beer in Trey's locker earlier that week, and that very morning Jennifer was sure she'd smelled alcohol on Trey's breath.

"He's only fifteen, Mrs. Fitch," Jennifer had said tightly, restraining her anger. "Where is he getting alcohol at eight o'clock in the morning?"

"Probably out of his mother's refrigerator or liquor cabinet," Annabel Fitch replied, not seeming at all surprised. "The gossip hotline says that the greatest thing she and her new boyfriend have in common is drinking."

Jennifer felt an upsurge of familiar frustration. She'd never become used to the callousness with which some parents treated their children.

"Dear God," she murmured, furious and sick at heart. The untapped potential in Trey had called up every protective instinct in her teacher's heart and everything within her rebelled at the waste of all the bright promise of his young life.

She leaned forward in her chair, her slim body taut with conviction. "Mrs. Fitch, Trey is one of the brightest students in my class, but he's flunking. He has to be tutored this summer if he's going to advance with his classmates in the fall. If he continues this pattern, he's going to be in a juvenile institution before he can graduate."

The principal nodded. "He reminds me a great deal of another student of mine—very intelligent, but with abominable home conditions. Of course, that was quite a few years ago."

Jennifer eyed the fond smile that softened Mrs. Fitch's stern features. "Did he end his life in prison?" she asked, certain that she already knew the answer.

"No," Annabel replied. "No, as a matter of fact, he became a pillar of the community."

Startled, Jennifer stared at the older woman. "How?" she demanded. "What happened? What did you do?"

"Me?" Annabel lifted an eyebrow. "I didn't do anything—he did it all."

"Well, then, what did *he* do? Perhaps we can find a way to get Trey to do the same thing."

"You know," Annabel said slowly, "you may have something there." She leaned her forearms on the polished desktop and eyed Jennifer. "I was Lucas Hightower's English teacher, just as you are Trey's. His father had a drinking problem, just as Trey's mother does. Lucas was too smart for his own good and he was using that intelligence to find new and inventive ways to get into trouble. I was at my wits' end when one of the local ranchers, a bachelor, requested that the school recommend a likely young man to work for him as a hired hand."

"And you gave him Lucas?" Jennifer guessed.

"I gave him Lucas," Annabel agreed. "Wayne Scanlon was a hard man, but he instilled in Lucas purpose and direction, and a love for the land that refocused his whole life. More important, he gave Lucas an example of how a man should live, and he made a home at the Lazy H for Lucas and his younger brother, Josh, after their father died. He was as proud of those boys as if they were his own sons. When Wayne passed away several years ago, he left the ranch to Lucas and Josh."

"If we could find a rancher to hire Trey to work during the day," Jennifer said reflectively, "and if I could convince him to study with me in the evenings... Summer vacation is only two weeks away and

Trey will have three months with too much time on his hands and too little to do except get into trouble. But if he has a job, and schoolwork, he won't have time to come up with any schemes for mischief, much less carry them out.''

That was when Annabel decided to enlist Lucas Hightower's help. Jennifer wasn't at all sure that Trey would agree to the plan. But Annabel had seemed confident. ''Trey will fall all over himself at the chance...there isn't a teenager in this county who doesn't hero-worship Lucas.''

''Really?'' Jennifer asked. ''Why?''

''Because Lucas Hightower is a local hero. He was a professional rodeo rider when he was younger, and he still wins most of the local rodeos.''

''Oh,'' Jennifer said politely. Although she was aware that many teenagers had heroes, she had never really understood the phenomenon. As a teen herself, she'd seen more than her share of charming men. Her mother had had a steady stream of them—and none of them had been anything but trouble and heartbreak. ''I see.''

''I doubt it.'' Annabel eyed the younger woman's blank expression and smiled. ''But you will.''

The noise of a car engine sounded in the empty parking lot outside, startling Jennifer from her reverie and back to the present.

She left the blackboard to peer expectantly out the window but saw only Butte Creek High School's algebra teacher, Louella Jackson, leaving for the day. The only cars remaining in the lot were Mrs. Fitch's blue sedan and Jennifer's own little red sports car, sitting in solitary splendor on the far side of the lot.

Jennifer remained at the window for several moments, her gaze lingering on the view. Sunlight poured through the bank of high windows that made up one whole wall of the classroom where Jennifer taught English. Now, in late May, the fields behind the school were a clear, spring green with shoots of growing wheat.

Jennifer sighed. Butte Creek, Montana, was dramatically different from her apartment in the Queen Anne district of Seattle, Washington, and the high school where she had taught for six years. Sometimes she felt she knew exactly how Alice must have felt when she tumbled down the rabbit hole. There was no question, however, that the job opening in the northeastern Montana ranching community had been heaven-sent. Burned out by the stress of teaching in the inner-city school and ready for a change, Jennifer had snapped up her principal's suggestion that she take a temporary job in the woman's hometown of Butte Creek.

"I might as well finish writing tomorrow's lesson on the board and go home to do my laundry," she murmured with exasperation when a last glance over her shoulder revealed a quiet, empty parking lot. "Lucas Hightower is obviously not going to keep his appointment with Mrs. Fitch."

Open book in hand, she slipped her reading glasses down from their perch atop her head and onto the bridge of her nose while she walked back to the blackboard. Jennifer located the chapter, scene and line she needed from *Macbeth* and began to write once again. The only sound in the quiet room was the slight scratch of chalk against blackboard.

* * *

Lucas parked his truck on the street in front of the high school and took the two concrete steps to the double doors in one long stride. The heavy doors gave easily under his hand and he stepped into the hallway. To his left stretched the wing that housed the elementary grades, and to his right was the L-shaped hall that made up Butte Creek's small high school.

He turned right, a wave of bittersweet memories hitting him as he breathed deeply and drew in the forgotten scents of school days. Each stride he took echoed in the empty halls and he automatically stepped more softly as he moved down the hallway. The doors to classrooms stood open on each side of the locker-lined hall. Lucas flicked a cursory glance into each room as he strode past. He'd rounded the corner and was halfway to the end of the hall and the principal's office, when his glance found an occupant. He stopped abruptly, his stunned gaze narrowing consideringly before he moved slowly to the doorway.

I'll be damned. His lips pursed in a soundless whistle. *Where the hell did she come from?*

A woman was standing with her back to him, holding a book in one hand while she wrote on the blackboard with the other. Red-gold hair was pulled back into an intricate braid. Silky curls escaped the vibrant, silky rope of hair that fell past the collar of her long-sleeved white blouse to reach halfway down her back.

Lucas's gaze moved lower, over the slender lines of her back to the narrow, belted waistband of a straight caramel-colored skirt. The skirt smoothed over the outward flare of slim hips and thighs but, unfortunately for Lucas, her legs were blocked from his view by the square, solid lines of the desk she stood behind.

The slight scratch of chalk against blackboard ceased and she glanced sideways at the book in her hand. Lucas's interest shifted from low gear to high. Behind the narrow black frames of reading glasses, her long lashes were lowered as she frowned over the book; the short, straight line of her nose was marred by a tiny bump on the bridge. Her lips moved, mouthing the words as she silently read a line to herself before she turned back to the blackboard.

She stretched to reach the far edge of the blackboard and Lucas's eyes narrowed. He was suddenly impatient to see what the woman looked like from the front; he definitely liked what he saw of her backside.

"I hope that whatever you're staring at is worth staying after school."

Her words carried a brisk warning, and Lucas jerked in reaction. He could have sworn the teacher had had no idea that he was watching her.

"Excuse me," he drawled, his deep voice loud in the quiet room. "I wonder if you could help me?"

The unfamiliar adult male voice wasn't the teenage tenor that Jennifer had been expecting. The sidelong glimpse she'd caught of a tall, jeans-clad form at the door had led her to believe that one of her students had been staring at her.

She looked over her shoulder, her gaze widening as she took in the cowboy in her doorway. His tall, broad body nearly filled the opening. He was dressed in boots, clean faded jeans, a blue work shirt with the cuffs of the long sleeves folded up over powerful forearms and a black Stetson over his crow-black hair. The hat's brim was tugged low to rest just above the black slash of his eyebrows, and beneath them, deep turquoise eyes watched her with unreadable intensity.

Jennifer felt the tiny hairs on the back of her neck rise and every survival instinct she owned went on instant alert. This man wasn't one of the mild-mannered, easily discouraged males she habitually cultivated as friends. He exuded confident strength and a dangerous sensual appeal. She stiffened, drawing herself up to her full five foot six, and frowned at him. ''You startled me!''

''Sorry, I didn't mean to.'' Lucas shifted, staring at the prickly woman. He decided the front view of gold eyes and a lush pink mouth set in a fine-boned face was every bit as good as her backside. His gaze flicked lower. *Yeah, definitely as good as the rear view,* he thought with appreciation. ''I'm looking for Mrs. Annabel Fitch.''

''Oh.'' Jennifer eyed the dangerous-looking man with barely concealed dismay. ''You must be Lucas Hightower.''

''Yes, ma'am.''

Removing her glasses, Jennifer carefully closed the book of Shakespeare. His unblinking, steady stare was beginning to make her nerves shiver and she resented his effect on her. She'd never been intimidated by men—in fact, the opposite had been true. Most of the men she met were put off by her self-contained life and dedication to her career. And she'd purposely, carefully, limited her male friends to only those men who posed no emotional threat to her well-ordered life.

No, she thought, she didn't like the fact that Lucas Hightower rattled her usually unshakable composure. She returned his stare with a cool, challenging glance. "Mrs. Fitch is waiting for you in her office. I'll take you there."

Lucas could have told her he knew the way to the principal's office, but he didn't. It was obvious that she'd taken an immediate dislike to him the moment he told her his name. He was damned if he knew why, but it irritated the hell out of him.

He stepped to one side to let her precede him into the hall. She moved smoothly, with a natural grace and economy of movement that was a pleasure to watch. As she passed him, the subtle scent of her perfume reached out to tease his nostrils.

Lucas racked his brain to remember what he'd heard about a new teacher at the school. He vaguely recalled the postmistress chattering about the English teacher leaving to have a baby. Something she'd told him about the replacement teacher nagged at his memory, but he couldn't quite place it.

"You're new here," he commented, slanting her a sideways glance. He wasn't sure why he was making small talk; he never made small talk with women. But he didn't have any trouble recognizing the signals his hormones were sending to his brain. What surprised him was their refusal to listen to his mind's automatic rejection. He also wasn't too happy with the fact that he noticed little things about her, like how long her eyelashes were, how creamy her skin looked and how she had skittered away from him like a cautious filly from a snaking rope when she'd brushed past him.

His deep drawl stroked shivers up Jennifer's spine, adding to the tension that hummed along her nerves. He was too big, too male and too close. She fought down the urge to put more space between them and chanced a glance at him, only to find that amazing turquoise gaze fastened on her. "Yes," she responded, the word carefully polite, concise and professional. "I am new. I was hired to complete the term when Mrs. Jenkins's baby arrived early."

"Mmm," Lucas murmured. She'd thrown up a wall of ice between them that felt ten feet thick. She clearly didn't want to talk to him. Perversely, he decided he did want to talk to her. "Where are you from?"

"Seattle. Here we are." Jennifer halted in front of the door to Mrs. Fitch's office and tapped on the wooden frame.

"Come in."

Lucas leaned around her and turned the knob to push the door inward. At five foot six, Jennifer rarely felt intimidated by a man's height. But Lucas Hightower was not only over six feet tall, he was quite simply a big man, with broad shoulders, deep chest and muscled arms. Never before had she been quite so aware of the differences between male and female. She resented the fragile, subtly threatened way his sheer size made her feel.

Jennifer drew in a deep, steadying breath and with it, the heady scent of soap, spicy after-shave and man. Irritated by her inability to ignore him, she stepped quickly past him and into the office.

"Lucas!" Annabel Fitch greeted her favorite ex-student warmly.

"Afternoon, Mrs. Fitch." Lucas took off his hat, his smile echoing the pleasure evident in his drawled greeting.

Jennifer felt her breath catch. Lucas Hightower's smile transformed the hard lines of his face from stern good looks to heart-stopping handsomeness. His deep blue eyes warmed with affection as he stepped forward and leaned across the desk. Mrs. Fitch's gnarled fingers disappeared in his grip when he enfolded her hand in his much larger palm.

"What was so important that you had to see me in person?" he asked with curiosity, eyeing the principal's diminutive figure. "Don't tell me those bleachers Josh and I built for the gym are worn-out already?"

"No, of course not, they're every bit as sturdy as when you set them up. Sit down." Annabel waved him to a seat and watched as he dropped onto the oak chair next to Jennifer. "I have a favor to ask of you and I felt it was best that I ask it in person."

"Really?" Lucas raised an eyebrow. He propped one ankle on the opposite knee and dropped his hat on the floor beside his chair. "What kind of favor?"

"I have a student, a young man, who needs employment for the summer," Annabel began. "I'll be blunt with you, Lucas. This particular young man has a history of getting into trouble. However, Miss McCleary and I feel strongly that he deserves a second chance and that if you were willing to give him a job this summer, it could go a long way toward setting his feet on the right path."

Lucas didn't say a word. Not a muscle in his hard body moved, not a shift of expression crossed his face.

"Just so there's no misunderstanding," he said slowly, his drawl more pronounced, "are you asking me to hire somebody to mend fences, or are you asking me to be a stand-in daddy for the summer?"

"Maybe a little of both."

"That's not possible," he said tightly, his eyes narrowing over the spare, birdlike figure of the woman facing him. "I could use another hand this summer, but I'm not qualified to be anybody's father."

"Mr. Hightower," Jennifer interjected. "If you would only agree to give Trey a job this summer—"

Lucas stiffened, his glance moving with lightning swiftness from Annabel Fitch to Jennifer's intense, determined features before flicking back to the principal.

"Trey?" he interrupted. "Is this Trey Webber we're talking about?"

"Yes, Lucas," Mrs. Fitch confirmed.

Lucas cursed under his breath. "You're actually asking me to take Suzie Webber's son out to the Lazy H? You must be out of your mind, Annabel. Even if I agreed to have him, what makes you think she'd let him go?"

It was a measure of his loss of composure that he'd called her Annabel, instead of Mrs. Fitch. Annabel folded her hands on top of the desk and fixed him with a stern eye.

"I think Suzie Webber is so involved with her current boyfriend that she won't care who takes Trey for the summer. And I think there's a good chance that you'll take him because he's fifteen, his mother is drinking too much and his life is drifting. You could change that, Lucas, maybe only for a three-month summer, but the Lazy H might be the saving of that boy." Annabel paused for a moment, then said, "And I don't think you're the kind of man who would walk away from that possibility, regardless of past injuries."

Lucas held her clear-eyed, understanding gaze for a long moment. "You know what you're asking of me, don't you?"

"Yes, Lucas, I believe I do."

Abruptly, he thrust himself out of his chair and stalked to the window.

Jennifer stared at his broad back. His hands were shoved into his back pockets, and he held himself with a rigid tenseness that suggested tightly leashed, explosive emotion. She glanced at Mrs. Fitch, only to find her blotting suspicious moisture from the corner of one eye. Clearly, there was more going on here than a simple request for student employment.

"How's he doing in school?"

Lucas's brusque words broke the tense silence and Jennifer jumped.

"Jennifer is his homeroom and English teacher," Mrs. Fitch answered. "I'm sure she can answer that better than I can."

"Trey isn't doing well," Jennifer said evenly. "He'll need to go to summer school in order to move on with his class in the fall."

Lucas turned to look at her. "Summer school? How do you expect him to do that and work at the Lazy H?"

"Well . . ." Jennifer glanced at Mrs. Fitch for support and then back at the intimidating rancher. "I can tutor him at night and on the weekends."

Lucas snorted. "Lady, if he works for me, he'll be working from dawn to dusk, and often later, six days a week. He'll get a day off when it rains or when we have slack time."

"Oh." Jennifer blinked, taken aback at his rejection of her plan. She thought quickly. "In that case, maybe I can give him assignments and meet with him when it rains or he has a free day."

Lucas slowly crossed his arms across his broad chest. "And just how do you think he'll manage that, since he's only fifteen? He can't drive into town to school."

"Then I'll drive out to your ranch," Jennifer snapped. She could feel her cheeks heat as she struggled not to lose her temper.

"Great," he growled. "Then I'd have two of you underfoot." Lucas shot a hard look at Annabel. "This won't work."

"Yes, it will, Lucas," she replied calmly.

Lucas's implacable gaze met hers for one long moment, his features stern and unyielding. "If anybody but you were asking, Annabel Fitch . . ." He expelled his breath in an impatient sigh, then turned his hard blue stare on Jennifer.

"I'll talk to him," he said. The barely concealed antagonism on the teacher's face dissolved and her eyes lit with warm delight and hope, a smile curving the lush fullness of her mouth. An unfamiliar urge to smile back startled him and he glared at her. "But I'm not promising anything."

Her gold eyes blinked at him in slow surprise, that soft smile quickly disappearing.

"Excellent, Lucas," Annabel said briskly. "You talk to Trey, then give me a call. I'm sure Jennifer and I can work out a schedule to see that Trey's schoolwork is taken care of this summer."

"You'd better spend your time figuring out how you're going to talk Suzie Webber into letting her son work for me," he growled softly.

"You just talk to Trey," Mrs. Fitch said with imperturbable calm. "I'm sure you'll like the young man—he reminds me a lot of you at that age."

Lucas laughed shortly. "That's not exactly a recommendation, ma'am. If I remember right, the only one who could stand me when I was fifteen was you."

"And Wayne Scanlon," Mrs. Fitch said softly.

"Yeah," he drawled. "And Wayne Scanlon." His gaze flicked to Jennifer and back to Annabel. "I don't suppose either of you know where I might find Trey?"

"Of course," Jennifer said smoothly, her tone purposefully neutral. "He's scrubbing down the bleachers in the gym. He should be there for at least another hour."

Lucas eyed her calm expression. "And I don't suppose you'd care to tell me exactly what he did to earn the privilege of scrubbing the bleachers?"

"No," Jennifer replied without a twinge of remorse. She wanted the rancher to cooperate and she doubted that a recital of Trey's latest escapade would aid their cause. "I wouldn't. If he cares to tell you, that's another matter entirely."

Lucas shrugged, muttered something under his breath and strode across the room. He swept his hat from the floor without pausing and stalked to the door.

"I'm not making you any promises," he repeated grimly.

Then he stepped through the doorway, pulling the door shut behind him with ominous quietness.

Jennifer listened to the sound of his boot heels echoing down the hallway toward the gym until only quiet remained. Her mind buzzed with a hundred unanswered questions about the hard-eyed, handsome rancher and his connection with Trey and the boy's mother, Suzie.

Chapter Two

Lucas heard the rhythmic thud of a basketball against the wooden gym floor long before he reached the double doors at the end of the wide, deserted hallway. The boy was at the far end of the gym with his back to Lucas, dribbling the ball toward the basket and dodging imaginary opponents along the way.

Lucas stepped inside quietly. He shoved his hands into his jeans pockets, leaned against the white-painted wall just inside the door and watched.

Suzie Webber had remarried and left Butte Creek when Trey was barely six months old. In the years since, they'd lived in her hometown only for brief periods of time between marriages. This time, Lucas knew that Suzie and Trey had been back in Butte Creek for six months, but he hadn't seen them since their return. And because of Suzie's open hostility toward him, Lucas had seen Trey only once in all of his fifteen years—when he was only a few days old.

Lucas measured the boy's coordination and agility as he feinted right, then left, before racing under the basket to make a lay-up. The ball swished through the net and he caught it, spinning away to elude the ghosts of the opposing team.

He moves like Clay did, Lucas acknowledged bleakly. There were other similarities—like the rangy build that promised to someday fill out into broad shoulders and powerful strength. There was a haunting familiarity in the boy's profile as he turned toward Lucas, but then the illusion was gone. The thin, strong-boned, good-looking face he saw was Trey's and Trey's alone. His father's fifteen-year-old expression had never held the hard maturity that Trey's owned.

Lucas knew the instant the kid spotted him, for the boy's body stiffened, his fingers freezing the ball against his midsection. Even from the length of the basketball court, Lucas felt the impact of that blue stare. *He's got his father's eyes.* Pain shoved a dull knife between his ribs, straight into his heart. Still, he met Trey's gaze impassively, not moving a muscle as the teenager walked slowly toward him.

"Afternoon," Lucas said, his deep voice rumbling in the barnlike room.

"Hi." Trey stopped some fifteen feet away from Lucas, the basketball tucked under one arm, and stared at him without blinking.

"I'm looking for Trey Webber," Lucas said, registering the wary distrust that lay in the depths of the boy's eyes. Everything about the kid—from the shock of too-long blond hair that fell across his forehead, to the faded black T-shirt, ripped and faded blue jeans, worn high-top sneakers and the cocky half glare— shouted attitude. Bad attitude. He was too thin, and the skin beneath his eyes was smudged dark with weariness.

"Yeah?" the kid answered. "You've found him."

"My name's Hightower, Lucas Hightower." Lucas straightened away from the wall and held out his hand.

Trey stared at it for a long moment before wiping his palm down his jean-covered thigh and gripping Lucas's calloused hand with his. "I know who you are, I've seen you around. And I've heard people talk."

"Yeah?" A slight grin lifted the corner of Lucas's hard mouth.

"Yeah." Trey eyed the big man. "I've seen you ride, too—at the rodeo in Wolf Point last year."

"Mmm," Lucas growled in disgust. "Then you saw me eating arena dust when that big red sorrel dumped me."

"Nope, I missed that." Trey's mouth curved in a grin. "But I saw you team-rope with your brother— and you won."

"Hmm." Lucas acknowledged the comment, but his attention was focused on the smile that lit Trey's eyes and drove out the dark shades of hostility that lay beneath the cocky facade. Maybe there was more to this kid than good looks and scruffy clothes. For one brief moment, enthusiasm and admiration made Trey look almost fifteen—and so unbearably familiar that Lucas went still, his muscles tensing to endure the unexpected crash of pain that was as fresh as if its cause were only yesterday. He made up his mind with characteristic, decisive abruptness. "I'm hiring another hand this summer for the Lazy H," he said without preamble. "Mrs. Fitch tells me you might be interested."

Stunned shock wiped the smile from Trey's face, followed by a blaze of hope that was quickly erased and replaced by caution.

"I might be," Trey said tightly. His voice chose that moment to slip from tenor bravado to bass and he flushed a deep red. But his gaze didn't waver from Lucas's.

Lucas felt a fist grab his heart and squeeze. Had Wayne Scanlon seen that same mixture of ragged hope and stubborn pride in himself at fifteen that he read now in the youthful face of Trey Webber?

"The job pays minimum wage," he said gruffly. "Plus board and room. Starts the day school is out for the summer and ends when school starts in the fall." He looked at the sneakers on Trey's feet. "You know how to ride a horse?"

Trey nodded.

"You'll need boots—you can't ride in those. If you don't have any, we—"

"I ain't no charity case," Trey said, bristling, his hands clenching into fists at his sides.

Lucas lifted one eyebrow and met the boy's furious blue glare. "Never said you were," he told him mildly. "Like I started to say, if you don't have a pair of boots, there's probably a used pair at the ranch that'll fit you. If not, you can buy your own with your first paycheck." He folded his arms across his chest and stared at the boy. "You'll be doing everything from shoveling manure to digging postholes, and the hours are whatever I say they are. Sometimes you'll be working before sunup and won't be finished before sundown. And no alcohol. None.'' Lucas's face was as implacable as his harsh voice. "Do you want the job or not?"

"Yeah," he said hoarsely. "Yeah." The word came out louder and stronger this time. "I want the job, Mr. Hightower."

"Good." Lucas nodded decisively and turned. He paused to look back at Trey. "Your teacher says that you have to go to school this summer—says she'll tutor you. That all right with you?"

"Yeah—I mean, yes, sir, whatever you say."

"Good." Lucas smiled fleetingly and pulled open the door. He stepped halfway through before he paused again. "Mrs. Fitch thinks you're scrubbing down the bleachers. I figure she'll be down here to check on you in another half hour or so."

Trey shot a guilty glance over his shoulder at the deserted pail and mop on the far side of the gym. "I'll be done by then," he said.

"That'll make her happy," Lucas said noncommittally.

And then he was gone.

Lucas was halfway down the hallway to Mrs. Fitch's office, before he heard Trey's ear-splitting yell and the sound of a basketball being slam-dunked.

A slow grin creased his handsome face. "I guess that means he likes the idea," he mused aloud. He still wasn't sure why he'd offered the kid a job. Maybe it was because he just couldn't bring himself to refuse Mrs. Fitch, not after all she'd done for him. Maybe it was because something about Trey Webber reminded him of himself at fifteen. He didn't want to believe that it had anything to do with the hope in the teacher's gold eyes. And he refused to acknowledge that buried deep within him was a need to atone for Trey's lack of a father. If his soul also held a bone-deep yearning for forgiveness from the boy, Lucas ignored the possibility.

The last vestiges of his grin faded, to be replaced by a frown. Whatever the reason, he was damn sure he was going to be sorry he got involved in this.

He's frowning, Jennifer thought when Lucas returned after several agonizing moments. *Oh, no, he's going to refuse.* Disappointment clutched her heart.

Lucas's gaze flicked from Mrs. Fitch's expectant face to the teacher's tense features. "The kid has a job." The teacher's face lit with delight, her eyes glowing golden, her soft mouth curving in a smile that staggered his heart and temporarily jumbled his thoughts. He blinked once, slowly, and forced his mouth to form words. "If his mother allows it—and that's a mighty big *if.*" His deep voice grated in the quiet room.

"I'll talk to Suzie Webber." Mrs. Fitch's voice reflected absolute confidence and a steely determination. "She'll do the right thing."

"I have a hard time believing that anyone can make Suzie do the right thing," Lucas growled. "But if you can, I'll give Trey a job. But that's it, Mrs. Fitch." He gave her a hard look. "Just a job. I'm not signing on to be his daddy. I'm not cut out to be any kid's role model, especially not this kid. If you want a miracle for him this summer, you'd be better off praying for the angels to hand you one."

Before Annabel could respond, Lucas switched the force of his blue stare to Jennifer.

"And I don't know how the hell you're going to teach him this summer. I haven't got time to drive him to town every day."

"We'll work out something," Jennifer said, unable to keep the elation out of her voice. She'd never thought that angels arrived wearing boots, jeans and a handsome scowl, but Lucas Hightower was clearly the answer to a prayer. Whether he thought so or not. "Thank you so much, Mr. Hightower."

"Don't thank me yet, lady," Lucas growled with irritation. "Even if you get his mother to agree to let Trey work for me, there's no telling whether or not he's got what it takes to last out the summer."

"We'll cross that bridge when we come to it," she said firmly, refusing to be sidetracked by his obvious doubts.

"Yeah, maybe." Lucas looked unconvinced. He tugged the brim of his Stetson lower over his forehead and turned to Mrs. Fitch. "You'll call me after you've talked to Suzie Webber?"

Annabel nodded. "Of course."

"All right." He flicked one last searing, unreadable glance over Jennifer, said goodbye and left.

Once again, Jennifer listened to the sound of his boots as he strode swiftly down the hall. When the sound faded into silence, she drew a deep breath and looked at Mrs. Fitch.

"He'll do it," she said blankly, almost dazed from the force of his personality and the crackling awareness that had arced between them with that last glance.

"Yes." Mrs. Fitch allowed herself a small sigh of relief, the only indication that she hadn't been as sure of Lucas as she'd seemed. "Now all I have to do is convince Suzie Webber that she has to cooperate with our plan."

Jennifer's curiosity nudged her and she fought its pull and lost. "Mrs. Fitch, what's the connection between Trey's mother and Lucas Hightower? Why wouldn't she want Trey to work for him this summer?"

Mrs. Fitch hesitated, sighing heavily. "I'm not one to pass along gossip, Jennifer, especially when I'm not sure what really happened ... Suzie Webber believes she has cause to hate Lucas. All I know for sure is that Lucas and Trey's father, Clay, were inseparable throughout school, and afterward, they traveled the rodeo circuit together. Suzie dated Clay in high school and after she graduated, she joined them on the circuit. A few months later, she and Clay were married, and within a year, he was dead. The three of them were in southern Colorado at a rodeo when it happened. Suzie brought him home to be buried at Butte Creek. She was about six months pregnant, and when she became hysterical at the funeral and accused Lucas of killing Clay, most folks figured it was the grief talking. But I've always thought there was more to it—especially since she started drinking after Trey was born and she hasn't stopped since.

"It's my guess that only Lucas knows what really happened. But as far as I know, he's never talked about it. If he wants to tell you, he will."

It was three days before Annabel Fitch called Lucas. When he hung up the phone, he leaned back in his chair and stared at it for long moments.

"Damn," he said finally. "Suzie said yes. Who the hell would have ever thought the old lady could persuade that kid's mom?" *I should have known. After all, who the hell would have ever believed that Annabel could have talked me into offering Trey a job, in the first place?*

Lucas avoided involvement like the plague. When he was sixteen and his father was killed in a bar brawl, he'd vowed that his father's life was never going to be his. He'd never be a drunk, because he was never going to drink. And he'd never again be responsible for another human the way he'd been for his father, because he was never going to get involved. As far as he was concerned, the man who'd sired him had given him nothing but bad memories and a fierce determination to never live the kind of life that had caused his mother to leave them and his father to die.

And then Suzie Webber had destroyed Clay. At first, Lucas had wished it was him instead of his best friend who was buried in the small Butte Creek cemetery. As time passed, the high wall surrounding his heart had thickened and reinforced his distrust of women. With the exception of his brother, Josh, he'd promised himself that he would stay uninvolved in others' lives.

"Hell," he said in disgust and glared at the blank computer screen on top of his desk. "I suppose I'll have to go see the teacher." He knew that her name was Jennifer McCleary, but he stubbornly refused to call her anything so personal.

Behind her desk, Jennifer propped her chin on her hand and stared unseeingly out the window of her classroom. She still had to contact Lucas Hightower and had no idea how she was going to manage the logistics of tutoring Trey this summer. She wanted a solid, workable plan in mind before she talked to the rancher. He'd been so positive that there was no solution to the problem that she was determined to prove him wrong.

Lucas Hightower hadn't been far from her thoughts since his deep voice had startled her at the blackboard three days ago. The only good thing about it, she reflected, frowning at the cheery sunlight, was that she hadn't suffered from insomnia all week. Instead, she'd fallen asleep and dreamed—dreams dominated by the big rancher—and although she didn't remember details, she'd woken restless and edgy each morning.

Having a man she'd actually met walk through her dreams had never happened to her before. Faceless, unnamed, romantic heroes had populated her dreams on occasion, but never a living, breathing, human male.

There was no question that Lucas Hightower was trouble; she knew that the best thing she could do for her peace of mind was to never see him again. Just because she'd never before felt the powerful lure and overwhelming demand of physical attraction didn't mean that she couldn't recognize the symptoms.

God knows, I had enough demonstrations after watching Mother go through three husbands, she reflected. *And more than enough proof that seething hormones and sexual fascination are a woman's one-way ticket to emotional disaster.*

Unfortunately, because of Trey, it was unlikely that she could avoid Lucas Hightower.

Jennifer struggled with the problem all afternoon and into the evening. But try as she might, she couldn't avoid the fact that the best possible solution to tutoring Trey was for her to drive to the Lazy H. A move that would put her directly within Lucas Hightower's orbit. On his own turf and in harm's way.

"The only plus in this situation is that I doubt Mr. Hightower is going to be any more delighted to have me in his house every other night than I will be to be there," she said aloud. "In fact, he said I'd be underfoot—and he didn't sound pleased." A rhythmic thumping responded to her voice and she glanced over her shoulder, smiling. "Just because you love me, Beastie, doesn't mean all males do."

Stretched out on the rug in front of the stove, the huge chocolate-colored Labrador grinned up at her, his tongue startling pink against his dark fur. Clearly, the big dog didn't agree with her.

Jennifer draped the damp dish towel across her shoulder and squatted on her heels in front of him to ruffle the silky fur behind his ears. "That's okay with me... What woman needs more than one handsome dog to love her?"

Beastie replied with a low, deep-throated affection-ate sound, leaning into her hand with a look of su-preme contentment. Suddenly, he stiffened and swung his head alertly toward the front door. Then he surged to his feet, toppling Jennifer over backward.

"Hey," Jennifer complained as she got up. "Did you have to knock me over?"

The rap of knuckles on the front door echoed through the small house and Beastie's hackles rose, a menacing growl rumbling out of his throat.

"Quiet, Beastie," she lectured the dog. "it's prob-ably just one of the neighbors." She wrapped her fin-gers around the Lab's heavy black collar and moved quietly across the room to snap on the porch light. Outside, the shadowy figure of a man loomed, broad-shouldered and massive. She knew only one man big enough to cast that shadow. Lucas Hightower was outside her door—and she wasn't at all sure that she was ready to see him.

Lucas shifted from one booted foot to the other, a frown growing. *What the hell is she doing in there?* he thought irritably. He'd heard a dog growl, and the porch light had flicked on in response to his knock, and then nothing. Seconds ticked by. He knocked again.

Chains rattled and locks clicked free. The door swung inward and the teacher, holding on to the col-lar of the biggest brown Labrador dog Lucas had ever seen, stood just inside.

She was barefoot, wearing some kind of stretchy, clinging gray pants with a loose, matching T-shirt that ended at midthigh. Her hair wasn't bound in a braid, but fell free halfway to her waist, framing her pale face in a riot of silky red-gold curls. Pale gold freckles dusted the fair skin of her nose and the high arch of delicate cheekbones, and her dark gold eyes held wary surprise.

"Mr. Hightower," Jennifer said politely. Beastie chose that moment to snarl threateningly, and with relief, she tore her gaze from the rancher's. "Beastie," she scolded sternly. "Stop that and sit down. Sit."

The big dog sat back on his haunches, but he still eyed Lucas with distrust.

"I'm sorry." Jennifer looked back at Lucas, "Beastie is quite protective. Won't you come in?"

Lucas stepped over the threshold, removing his hat as he did so. Jennifer shifted back and the dog moved with her, still eyeing him with patent wariness.

"Big dog," he commented, noting the size of the dog's head and teeth when a silent snarl curled the animal's lip back from white incisors.

"Yes." Jennifer glanced down at the Lab and frowned at him. "Beastie," she commanded. "Stop that—he's a friend. Hold out your hand, Mr. Hightower."

"Why?" he said mildly. "Hasn't he had dinner yet?"

Startled, Jennifer looked up to find an amused twinkle in Lucas's eyes. She almost smiled back at him before she remembered that she didn't want their relationship to be more than politely friendly. Every instinct she owned told her to keep him at arm's length. She couldn't afford even one chink in her armor.

She was careful to keep her voice neutral. "I want him to sniff your hand while I'm holding him so that he knows I accept you and that he has permission to treat you like a friend."

"Ah," Lucas nodded in understanding and held out his hand slowly, palm up, toward the dog's nose. "In that case, I guess I can trust you to make him give my hand back."

"Of course," Jennifer answered promptly, her grip tightening on the dog's collar as he stretched his neck to sniff suspiciously at the rancher's palm. The two watched for a long moment until the dog relaxed, and his pink tongue flicked out to swipe with wet friendliness across Lucas's palm. "Oops, sorry about that." She released Beastie's collar and quickly offered Lucas the damp dish towel slung across her shoulder. "Here, use this. On second thought, why don't you come into the kitchen and wash?"

"All right." Lucas followed her through the living room, his swift, curious glance registering the bright serape covering the plain green of the overstuffed, old-fashioned sofa. The Mexican blanket's vivid reds, blues and greens were repeated in the plump solid-colored pillows strewn across the seat and tumbled onto the floor.

The teacher had transformed the rented house's white-painted walls and ordinary, bland furnishings with brilliant splashes of color, irrevocably stamping the room with a personality that was as vivid as her mane of strawberry-blond hair.

Ignoring the urge to stop beside her bookcase and read the titles of the books and CDs, Lucas stepped into the kitchen, and paused behind Jennifer when she halted in front of the sink.

"I should have remembered that licking your hand is his way of saying he accepts you," Jennifer said over her shoulder as she turned on the tap. She handed him a bar of soap and stepped aside while he rolled up the sleeves of the white, pearl-snapped shirt he wore and washed his hands.

"Would you like a cup of coffee?" she offered. "I just brewed a fresh pot."

"Sure—thanks." Lucas turned off the water and picked up the towel, leaning against the counter and watching her while he dried his hands.

"I assume you're here to talk about Trey," she said, stretching to reach the shelf above the stove and collect two mugs.

"Yeah," Lucas said absently, his gaze following the stretch of gray cotton over the smooth curve of hip and leg. Long legs, slender and shapely. He shook himself and turned to hang the wet towel over the rack beside the sink. "Mrs. Fitch called—Trey will be working for me this summer. Have you figured out how you're going to have him do schoolwork?"

"I have a plan." Jennifer finished pouring coffee into the mugs and turned to find him watching her with a disconcerting intensity. "Why don't we sit down?"

Lucas held her chair while she set the mugs on the table before seating herself.

His old-fashioned politeness flustered Jennifer. She hadn't been expecting it and in the brief moment before he moved away from behind her, she swallowed her instinct to put the length of the room between them. She didn't trust the elemental, electric reaction she felt every time she was in the same room with him. It was almost as if he used up all the available oxygen, charging the air around him with dangerous energy and leaving her faintly breathless. She sipped her coffee and eyed him warily while he settled into the chair opposite her and cradled his own steaming mug in his hands. His powerful forearms and the backs of his hands were dusted with fine, dark hair, the palms and fingers callused, his fingernails close-trimmed and clean.

For the life of her, she couldn't remember finding a man's hands and arms fascinating before, let alone thinking they were sexy. Weren't women supposed to be turned on by broad shoulders and muscles? Of course, she thought with irritation, he had those, too.

She yanked her thoughts away from Lucas Hightower's hands and shoulders with ruthless determination.

"Because of the distance involved, I think it would be best if I drove out to your ranch to tutor Trey in the evenings," she began with a brisk firmness that she hoped would set the tone for their discussion. "Perhaps every other evening and maybe Saturday or Sunday afternoon, if he's free on the weekend."

Lucas frowned.

"I know it will inconvenience you," she said quickly, afraid that he was going to refuse. "But frankly, I can't think of a better plan."

Lucas shook his head and took a sip of coffee. "It won't be inconvenient," he said finally, reluctantly. "You can use the table in the living room for your books—it'll be quieter there than in the bunkhouse."

"Good." Jennifer released her held breath with relief and smiled brilliantly, unaware of the effect it had on the man sitting opposite her. "That's settled then. I'll drive out the first Monday after school vacation starts, shall we say around six-thirty or seven?"

"That should be fine," Lucas agreed, still recovering from the impact of her smile. She had a tiny dimple at the corner of her mouth that flashed when she smiled and he fought the urge to test its depth with the tip of his forefinger. He drew his wandering thoughts back with an iron hand. "Has he been behaving himself?"

"Actually, yes," Jennifer said. Relief that he'd accepted her plan so easily made her forget that she'd decided to keep as much distance as possible between herself and Lucas. She tucked an errant curl behind her ear and leaned forward. "I think this plan of ours has a chance of working. He hasn't been in any trouble since you offered him the job. And he came to talk to me earlier today about studying this summer— clearly, he's willing to cooperate. I have to thank you for that."

"Why?" Lucas was a little confused.

"Trey believes that his job with you includes cooperating with me and being tutored this summer."

"I didn't tell him that." Lucas shook his head, his deep voice emphatic. "What the kid does about school is up to him. All I told him was that I'd work his tail off this summer. Period."

"Hmm," Jennifer stared at his impassive expression. Lucas seemed adamant that he wasn't going to be responsible for Trey in any role except that of an employer. "Well, Trey seems to think it would please you if he studied this summer, and whether or not you meant him to believe it, I'm glad he does. It will make my job that much easier if he's studying because he wants to and not because I'm forcing him."

"That's good then," Lucas said, his voice unconsciously softening as he noticed her animated face, her cheeks pinkened with color, her golden eyes glowing with enthusiasm. "You really care about the kid, don't you?"

"Yes, of course I do," she answered, distracted by the stroke of the intimate, deepened bass of his voice and the blue heat in his eyes. His gaze flickered lower to fasten on her mouth and she shivered in reaction, her tongue unconsciously moving to lick suddenly dry lips. The air in the room thickened with tension, awareness pulsing between them. Dazed, Jennifer thought she heard the crackling of electricity.

Lucas read the stunned response and shocked dismay in her face and nearly groaned aloud at his body's instant, demanding answer.

"This isn't going to work," he muttered. He knew damn well that he didn't want to get involved with her. She didn't look like the type for a short, hot affair with no ties. Still, the sudden urge to lean forward and press his mouth to her soft, pale skin almost had him giving in to temptation. He shoved his chair back abruptly and stood.

"I better be going," he said tightly, and grabbing his Stetson from the table, he strode out of the room.

Jennifer stared at the empty chair for a long second before she jumped up and followed him. He had his hand on the doorknob, and was turning it, but nothing happened.

Lucas stared blankly at the recalcitrant door before he realized that it wasn't opening. Behind him, he heard Jennifer's quick footsteps.

"You have to release the dead bolt," she said, the slight, breathy catch in her voice telling him she wasn't immune to that tense moment in the kitchen.

Lucas fought the urge to turn around, pin her soft curves against the wall and find out if her mouth tasted as good as it looked. He didn't know which irritated him the most—her, for causing this itch, or his own rebellious body for being stupid enough to go up in flames every time he got within ten feet of her. He couldn't ever remember getting this turned on by a woman he hardly knew, and he resented the hell out of her for making him ache.

He cursed himself silently and turned the brass knob to pull the door inward.

Chapter Three

Lucas stopped and turned to look back at her. "I meant what I said when I told you that the kid's studying doesn't have anything to do with his job. If he can't cut the work, I'll fire him, just the same as I would any other hired hand. And the work comes first—if you keep him up late studying, he still has to roll out of bed in the morning and put in a full day's work."

Jennifer stiffened at his grim, implacable tone and her eyes narrowed. "You may not have any confidence in Trey, Mr. Hightower, but I do. I'm sure he's capable of handling both the job and his studies."

"I hope you're right," he said slowly, studying the stiff lines of her body and the barely hidden irritation in her eyes. The wall of ice was back. "But he's a town kid. If he lasts a month, I'll be surprised." He stepped out onto the porch. "Good night, Teacher."

"Good night," Jennifer responded. She moved forward, curling her fingers around the edge of the open door.

Lucas looked at her, reluctant to leave. The lamp-light from the living room backlit her slender figure, turning her red-gold curls into living fire and sculpting shadows beneath her cheekbones and jaw. She seemed fragile and vulnerable, even with the big dog seated at her side and the lock on the door.

"I'll expect you the first Monday after school gets out," he said abruptly.

"Right," Jennifer answered. Her eyes met his with clear, unspoken challenge. "I'll be there."

His gaze left her face and flicked to the dog. The Labrador's ears lifted alertly and he immediately began to wag his tail.

Lucas wanted to tell the teacher to stay away from the Lazy H and out of his life, but he'd backed himself into a corner by agreeing to hire Trey for the summer. The two were a package deal. Still, he hesitated and was immediately irritated by his reluctance to leave her. "Good night." He forced his feet to move and turned to leave her porch and lawn for the relative security of his truck. He didn't even break his stride when he heard her call a final good-night behind him; he just lifted a hand in acknowledgment.

He heard the door close as he reached his pickup and by the time he'd yanked open the truck door and slid behind the wheel, she'd switched off the porch light.

She's trouble.

The knowledge plagued him down every one of the thirty miles between Butte Creek and home.

Jennifer continued to stare out the window long after Lucas was gone.

This is unbelievable, she thought, finally turning away from the closed door.

She'd seen Lucas Hightower exactly two times, and both times he'd stirred more heat with one long, penetrating look than any kiss she'd ever shared with any other man. Furthermore, she didn't seem to be able to stop her body's reaction; it was like being blindsided by a semi.

She'd thought she was immune to passion.

She was wrong.

"This isn't good, Beastie," she said to her dog. She paused to turn on the CD player and the gravelly voice of Louis Armstrong rasping out the lyrics to "Beale Street Blues" followed her into the kitchen. "This is no time to meet a man who makes my libido go haywire. I've got enough problems dealing with Trey. I haven't got time to cope with my first real case of raging hormones."

Beastie sat on his haunches and watched with interest as she carried the empty coffee mugs from the table to the sink. His ears pricked up and he cocked his head when she turned and shook a spoon at him.

"And that's all this is—hormones. It can't be anything else. I hardly know the man." She turned and dropped the spoon into the dishwater. "Besides, Mother had three hasty marriages and three children—all of whom were the direct result of lust and hormones." She eyed the Lab with disapproval. "I decided years ago that I'd be much more sensible. And that's exactly what I'm going to be. Sensible. And I'm going to keep as much space between me and Lucas Hightower as possible.''

Her hands ceased their movements in the dishwater and she frowned at Beastie. ''Just exactly how I'm going to do that, I don't know,'' she said slowly, ''considering I just agreed to go to his house several times a week all summer long.''

She finished washing the two coffee mugs and tipped them upside down on the drainboard to dry. The image of Lucas's big hands wrapped around the heavy blue mug flashed into her mind and she determinedly forced it into a corner and locked it away. Lucas Hightower wasn't for her; only a fool knowingly walked into fire.

The map Mrs. Fitch had drawn for Jennifer was simple, clear and direct. Thirty miles of county road led her straight to the Lazy H.

Jennifer slowed her sports car to a crawl and squinted against the lowering sun to see the square, black letters painted on the side of a large metal mailbox. The big box stood in solitary splendor on the wide shoulder of the road, its solid, square post marking the entrance to a long lane. At the far end of the narrow ranch road, tucked up against the base of sheltering buttes, a cluster of buildings was just visible. A grove of trees, the rancher's standard barrier against the winds that scoured the prairie, stood in a green curve behind the buildings.

''Hightower,'' Jennifer read aloud. ''This has to be the right place.''

She turned off the county road and onto a graveled lane. Green wheat fields stretched to her left, and on the right, fenced pasture land dipped and rolled, slowly easing upward until the acres merged with the half circle of buttes that cradled the ranch buildings in their curve.

Jennifer braked to a halt in front of the house. Lucas's home was a white, two-story, rambling structure with a wide porch that reached across the front. The big yard surrounding it boasted two large box elder trees that shaded the sparse grass and brushed the sides and roof of the house with outstretched, leafy limbs. Trees were rare on the prairie; clearly, some early homesteader had planted and lovingly nurtured the big old trees.

"Hello—is anyone home?" There was no answer to either her knock or her call. She turned and surveyed the buildings. Beyond the house fence was an open area nearly half the size of a football field. On her far left stood a huge red barn with corrals extending off both sides. A low-roofed, three-sided cattle shed made up the back side of the farthest corral. There were four other outbuildings; beyond them stretched fenced pastures where a half-dozen horses grazed.

Puzzled, she waited for another ten minutes before she returned to her car, leaned through the rolled-down window and honked the horn. The resulting noise startled a bay horse from the cattle shed next to the barn, but his responsive whinny was the only answer to the horn's demand.

Jennifer glanced at her watch and frowned.

"Seven o'clock," she said. "Where can they be? Lucas agreed that I should be here between six-thirty and seven o'clock on the first Monday after summer vacation began.''

Her gaze searched the length of the lane to the road, but it was empty. She turned in a half circle, scanning the fields and then the pastures behind the house where a dirt track wound away across the coarse grass and disappeared around the bulge of a butte.

She walked slowly back to the porch, dropped into a worn oak rocking chair, and prepared to wait.

Jennifer rocked back and forth; the easy, soothing motion, combined with the quiet peacefulness of the ranch and the warm evening air, lulled her into drowsy half wakefulness.

The minutes ticked lazily by, and it was seven-thirty before the sound of engines broke the evening stillness. Jennifer stirred, pushed up out of the comfortable chair and leaned out across the railing to search for the vehicles. She was rewarded with the sight of two pickup trucks rounding the far butte, dust puffing up behind their wheels as they raced across the flat. They disappeared for a few moments when the road dipped into a coulee, but they quickly reappeared and a short five minutes later, they braked to a halt in front of the house.

A swift surge of unfamiliar, unwelcome excitement flooded Jennifer when she recognized Lucas behind the wheel of the first pickup. Ruthlessly, she clamped down hard on the instinct that nearly propelled her down the steps to greet him.

Fortunately, Trey's slim, dusty form jumped to the ground from the bed of the second, older pickup and claimed her attention. She smiled at the teenager, refusing to look at Lucas as he stepped out of his truck.

Three more men piled out of the trucks and began to unload equipment from the back of the second pickup.

Lucas's long strides slowed at the base of the steps, before he took them two at a time to reach her.

"Sorry we're late." He pulled off his Stetson and wiped his forehead with the back of his wrist before settling the hat back on his head. He hoped to God the sheer, gut-deep relief he felt at seeing her standing on his porch didn't show on his face. "A pump broke down in the north pasture and it was a bi—a bear to fix."

Jennifer smiled politely. "I'm sorry, I hope you didn't stop work just because I'm here. I didn't mind waiting."

Before Lucas could respond, Trey's voice interrupted them.

"Hi, Miss McCleary." He trotted up the walk and halted at the foot of the steps.

"Hello, Trey." A genuine smile curved her mouth as she looked down at the teenager. His thin face was dirty and, like Lucas's, it was smudged with black grease, but a glow of contentment lurked behind the usual wary caution in his eyes.

Two older men and one younger approached, halting behind Trey to stare curiously at Jennifer.

"Well, now." The drawled words came from one of the older men. Whip-thin, his long bowed legs were encased in faded blue stovepipe jeans, and the faint stubble on his cheeks and jaw was as white as the snowy hair visible beneath his worn-out gray cowboy hat. He grinned at Jennifer, his black eyes twinkling. "If you ain't a sight for sore eyes, ma'am." He nodded his head at Lucas. "I keep tellin' the boy, here, that a man needs a pretty woman to come home to at night."

The old man's Southern drawl and blatant flirting had Jennifer smiling with amusement. Beside her, Lucas gave a snort of disgust.

"Shut up, Murph," he growled without heat, "and stop trying to charm the teacher—she's here to tutor Trey, not to listen to you spin a line."

Clearly unconcerned by Lucas's words, Murph grinned unrepentantly and winked at Jennifer.

"Miss McCleary, this old buzzard is Murphy Redman." Lucas paused as Murphy limped up the steps and took Jennifer's hand in his. "And this is Charlie Allen."

The grizzled cowboy who next claimed her hand with brief, solid pressure was shorter and heavier than Murphy, but his blue eyes were just as keen, and his hair just as white.

"Pleased to meet you, Miss McCleary," he said politely.

"It's nice to meet you, Mr. Allen," she responded.

"And this is my brother, Josh," Lucas said.

Jennifer's gaze moved past Charlie and clashed with a hard aqua-blue stare only a shade lighter than Lucas's. He took her outstretched hand with a brief, hard grip.

"Miss McCleary." His tone was perfunctory, his words emotionless.

"Mr. Hightower," Jennifer said politely. He immediately released her hand and turned away. She glanced curiously at Lucas. A faint frown creased his forehead as the screen door slammed behind Josh. For a moment, anger roiled with worry in his blue eyes; then all emotion was wiped from his expression.

"We're running late," he said abruptly. "We'll throw something together for dinner and then you and Trey can get to work in the living room."

"I'm starvin'," Murph declared, pulling open the screen door and stepping back. "After you, ma'am." He bowed and ushered her through the door ahead of him.

Jennifer's quick glance registered a wide entrance hall with an open staircase down one side. Across from it, a double-wide doorway gave her a glimpse of a long living room.

"The kitchen's this way." Lucas gestured ahead of her.

She preceded the men down a wide hallway to the back of the house and stepped into a large, square kitchen. High windows flooded the room with light and a door to a utility porch on the far side stood ajar.

"Coffee's ready," Josh's deep voice said briefly. He stood with his back to the room, pouring coffee into a mug from a large, timer-set electric coffeemaker on the countertop near the sink.

"Great," Murph said with satisfaction. "You want some coffee, Miss McCleary?"

"I'd love some," Jennifer answered. "And it's just Jennifer, please."

"Right." Murphy was reaching for a mug, when he suddenly stopped. "Oh, hell," he said in disgust and glanced apologetically at Jennifer. "I'm filthy—I reckon you better come get your own mug."

"All right." Jennifer crossed the room, took a mug from the rack on the wall and filled it. She sipped it as she turned, and found five pairs of male eyes watching her expectantly. At the sink, water ran unheeded over Lucas's soapy hands while he stared at her. She halted abruptly, swallowing the mouthful of coffee and frantically trying to think what social error she'd committed. "What?" she asked warily. "Is something wrong?"

Chapter Four

"How's the coffee?" Lucas asked, his voice dry, his blue eyes weighing her.

"Fine." Jennifer watched the quick exchange of disbelieving looks and the lifted eyebrows. Realization dawned and she repressed a grin. "Actually," she continued, "it's hot, black and strong enough to float nails. Just the way I like it."

"Well, I'll be damned," Murphy said softly, a grin creasing his lined face. "If that don't beat all! Most women choke like you've fed 'em poison the first time they taste Lucas's coffee. How come you don't?"

"I'm from Seattle, where there's an espresso cart on every other corner. A Seattle double shot latte is so strong that sometimes you can't drink it, you have to chew it."

"No kiddin'?"

Jennifer laughed. "Well, actually, maybe it's not quite that strong, but it's close."

"Never been to Seattle," Charlie commented. "I don't much like cities, but anyplace that makes good coffee can't be all bad."

Lucas grabbed a towel from a bar mounted on the counter and stepped aside to let Charlie wash. "You can use a table in the living room, Teacher." He nodded his head at the door across the room. "I'll show you. Trey, as soon as you're washed up, help Murphy get the stew on the stove."

He tossed the damp towel on the countertop next to the sink and waited for Jennifer to join him.

The four men in the kitchen moved smoothly through what clearly were chores they were accustomed to performing. Jennifer stepped into the living room, a large rectangular room with an open-beam ceiling and heavy, masculine furniture.

Lucas swept a stack of papers and magazines to one end of an old pedestal table, clearing half of the solid oak surface.

"This should give you enough room. If you need more, feel free to throw the magazines on the floor."

"Thank you," she said, wary of the impatience she sensed beneath the weariness etched on his face. "I'm sure this will be fine."

"Where are your books?" he asked, realizing for the first time that all she held was the coffee mug she'd filled in the kitchen. The late-evening sunlight slanted low through the window behind her, distracting him with the glimmers of gold it found in her red-blond hair. She wore it confined in a long braid and he felt a pang of regret that it wasn't loose, curling in a red-gold mass around her shoulders the way it had that night at her house. His fingers itched with the need to test just how soft and silky that smooth braid of red-gold was, and he closed them into fists to drive away the urge. It was bad enough that she was wearing worn, soft blue jeans that fit her curves like a second skin. The ordinary, loose-fitting white T-shirt was anything but ordinary where it draped over her breasts. He clenched his fists harder and dragged his thoughts back to her books.

"I left them outside, on a chair on the porch," Jennifer answered. He was staring at her with narrowed eyes, his expression hard, and she wondered uneasily if he was going to tell her to leave.

"I'll get them." He turned abruptly and left her. The front screen door had barely slammed behind him before he was back. "Here you go," he said, stacking the books next to her purse on the tabletop. "Make yourself comfortable—I'll send Trey in as soon as he's finished eating."

"Thank you," Jennifer said to his retreating back.

Her seat at the table gave her a clear view of the kitchen and she sipped her coffee and pretended to consult notes and a book while she surreptitiously watched the men. She was amazed at the swift efficiency with which they emptied huge cans of stew into a big kettle and left it to heat while they hauled out loaves of bread, butter and restaurant-size cans of peaches in syrup.

Even more astonishing was the speed with which the food disappeared once the men plunked the kettle down in the middle of the kitchen table and began eating.

"I sure am gettin' tired of beef stew," Murphy complained. He slathered butter a half-inch thick on a slice of bread and glanced at Lucas. "Where are we workin' tomorrow, boss? Maybe I can take off and come home to throw a roast and some potatoes in the oven in the afternoon."

"Sorry, Murphy." Lucas shook his head. "We have to fix fence on the north ranch and the generator's been acting up, probably needs to be overhauled. Not to mention the pump at the water well. We'll be lucky to get out of there before dark."

"Aw, hell," Murphy grumbled. "Maybe we should just drive on north to the border and eat at Red's Place."

Lucas shrugged. "Fine by me. Eating somebody else's cooking sounds like a good idea. I'm getting pretty sick of canned stew, myself."

Clearly, tonight's meal wasn't an unusual occurrence. Before Jennifer had time to more than shake her head in disbelief, the kettle was empty, bowls scraped clean and the men were pushing back their chairs.

"You don't have to clean the kitchen tonight, Trey," Lucas said, halting the boy when he began to scrape and stack plates and bowls. "The teacher's waiting for you."

When he clapped the teenager on the shoulder and gave him a gentle shove in her direction, Jennifer swallowed a start of surprise. Trey didn't shrug off Lucas's hand or jerk away from his touch. Not only did he allow the masculine gesture, but Jennifer could swear that the teenager flushed with pleasure.

"Yes, sir."

Trey's voice was neutral, but Jennifer was sure she didn't misread the quick flash of emotion in his eyes before he stepped toward her.

However, when he dropped into the chair opposite her at the table, his face was carefully blank.

"I'm ready, Miss McCleary. What are we doing tonight?"

"I thought we'd start with English and for the first few weeks, run through a refresher course in basic sentence structure and writing."

A long-suffering sigh met her answer. "Yes, ma'am." The resignation in Trey's voice was clear.

Jennifer ignored his lack of excitement. "And you need to brush up on your algebra," she continued.

"Yes, ma'am."

"And then, of course, there's stretching you on the rack and basic torture techniques," she said matter-of-factly.

"Yes, ma'am."

Jennifer eyed him with exasperation. "Trey, you haven't heard a word I said, have you?"

"Of course I have. You said we need to study English—sentences and writing."

Silence. "And?" Jennifer prompted.

"And—" he faltered, frowning at her in concentration. "And math—yeah, that was it. Math."

"It was algebra," she said wryly. "Are you sure you're up to this tonight?"

Trey shifted in his seat and cast a quick, sideways glance into the kitchen. Lucas was just closing the door on the dishwasher. He turned the knob and the resultant noise filled the room, spilling over into the living room where Trey and Jennifer sat. Trey's gaze followed Lucas as he turned and left the kitchen by the back door.

"Yeah," he said reluctantly. He squared his shoulders as he turned back to face Jennifer. "Studying is part of the deal."

"Very well." Jennifer recognized the determination on his face. "Then we'll go over a few basics and I'll leave you with assignments and books for Wednesday. And since we've started a bit late, we'll shorten tonight's session to an hour, all right?"

"Sounds good." Trey's voice held relief. He took the book she slid across to him.

"We'll start on page ten." She opened her own text before handing him paper and pencils. "You'll need these."

"Thanks." He flushed and flicked her an uncomfortable glance. "Sorry I'm not prepared."

"That's okay." She grinned in commiseration as he shifted and winced. "I imagine you're still getting used to early mornings and long days—and stiff muscles," she added.

"Yeah," he agreed. "Murphy shakes me awake before sunup. We do chores in the barn before breakfast and then we're gone the rest of the day. We're usually home sometime between five and six, though. Today was the first day that we got home this late."

"Do you always have dinner out of cans?" she asked, unable to stifle her curiosity.

Trey shrugged. "Usually. Once we drove into Butte Creek and ate at Stoke's Restaurant."

Jennifer frowned. Was it her imagination, or had his thin body grown even thinner in the last week?

"What do you do for lunch?"

"We pack sack lunches—sandwiches and stuff."

"Don't you get tired of canned food and bag lunches?" she asked.

"Nah." Trey shrugged in dismissal. "It's better than at home—at least there's something hot every night. I can't complain. Murphy said Lucas was gonna hire a cook, but all he could find was me—and I sure can't cook anything but eggs."

Jennifer hid her shock. Had Lucas sentenced his crew to a summer of canned and frozen food in order to take on Trey? If she hadn't asked him to help the boy, would he have hired a cook instead?

"So," Trey said, tapping a finger on the open page before him, "do I have to do the homework assignments at the end of the chapter or are you going to give me something different?"

"What? Oh, I thought we'd combine the two and target the areas you need to practice the most."

She leaned forward, forcing herself to concentrate on the English lesson.

An hour passed before Jennifer finished going over the last of Trey's questions. Doggedly determined as the teenager was to do his part, the droop of his shoulders gave away the weariness that dragged at him.

"Let's call it a night, Trey." She closed her textbook with finality. "You should be able to do the homework with what we've covered tonight. If not, we'll go over it again on Wednesday."

"Sure." His voice was noncommittal, but a quick flash of relief crossed his features. He closed his textbook and quickly gathered the small sheaf of papers he'd scribbled notes on.

Jennifer shook her head when he held out the pencils and unused paper. "Keep them, you're going to need them."

"Yeah." Trey ruefully acknowledged the amused twinkle of sympathy in her eyes. "I'm afraid you're right."

He shoved back his chair and stood, tucking the pencils into his back pocket and the sheaf of papers and stack of books under his arm. He hesitated. "I, uh, I guess I'll see you on Wednesday, then?"

"Yes." Jennifer pushed back her chair and stood, shuffling her papers and books into a stack. "I'll be here—don't forget to read the first five pages of Henry Thoreau's *Walden.*"

"I won't forget. Good night," he said before he turned and headed for the door.

The screen door slapped shut behind him, followed by the murmur of voices. Jennifer caught Trey's lighter tone, followed by a deeper bass that she recognized as Lucas's. She waited until she heard Trey's boots on the porch steps and then counted to ten before crossing the room.

Jennifer stepped through the screen door and paused, her gaze searching the darkness. Stepping from the lamplit living room into the darkness outside momentarily blinded her and she blinked, narrowing her eyes as her vision adjusted, until she located Lucas. He was a tall, broad form in the shadowy night and for a moment she hesitated, intimidated. Then she mentally squared her shoulders, lifted her chin and stepped toward him.

"Trey seems to be adjusting well," she said.

"He's doing all right," Lucas answered. The dark night surrounded them, enclosing them in intimacy. The soft glow of the lamplight that fell through the door behind her backlit her slender form. A breeze kicked up and whispered across the yard lot, rustling the leaves on the old box elders and teasing the soft cotton of Jennifer's T-shirt, flattening the white material against her breasts for a moment before it subsided. He tried to ignore the scent of her perfume carried by the breeze and yanked his gaze away from her body and back to her face. "He's got a lot to learn, but he's willing to try. That counts for a lot."

"I'm glad you're pleased with him. I wanted to thank you again for hiring him this summer—he told me that you would have hired a cook if you hadn't hired him."

Lucas shrugged, uncomfortable with her appreciation. "I wouldn't have hired him if I hadn't needed another hand, and sometimes we have a cook during the summer, sometimes we don't. It's no big deal."

"Still, I want you to know how much I appreciate what you're doing for him, and your allowing us the use of your home for his studies."

"Hell," Lucas growled. "He's earning his keep, and letting you use my table for a few hours doesn't exactly qualify me for sainthood."

Jennifer smiled; she'd never met anyone less saint-like than Lucas Hightower. "Perhaps not," she agreed, undisturbed by his refusal to accept her thanks. "But I appreciate your cooperation, nonetheless." She shifted her books and stared at him for a moment, but he was silent. Only the flare of his cigarette answered her, the tip glowing brighter as he drew on it, casting a brief red glow over the hard planes of his face and his shadowed, unreadable expression.

She glanced away from him and across the silent yard lot and dark outbuildings. "I'd better be going," she said. "I know you don't want my thanks, Mr. Hightower, but I truly appreciate what you're doing for Trey. I'll see you on Wednesday."

Without waiting for a reply, she quickly left the porch. She didn't look back until she was in her car pulling away from the house; when she did, his shadowy form still stood motionless on the porch, the red glow of his cigarette the only visible sign of life.

Two days later, Jennifer arrived at the ranch house at four o'clock in the afternoon. Lucas had made it abundantly clear that he didn't want her gratitude for his help with Trey, but she was just as determined to show her appreciation. She wasn't sure which was the strongest motivation for her plan: her unwillingness to owe a debt of gratitude to Lucas Hightower or her concern that Trey needed several hot, filling meals every week.

Whatever the true reason, she'd spent the afternoon indulging in one of her favorite hobbies—cooking. The trunk of her car was filled with the results: a huge beef roast with potatoes, onions, carrots and celery browned in the thick juice, a bowl of mixed green salad, biscuits and three apple pies still warm from the oven.

A quick glance around the quiet ranch told her that the men were gone, but she ran lightly up the porch steps and knocked on the screen door, anyway.

No one answered, and she pulled open the screen and twisted the doorknob of the heavy inner door. It gave easily under her fingers and she heaved a sigh of relief that it wasn't locked.

"Hello?" she called into the quiet interior of the house.

Silence answered her and she pushed the door wide and stepped inside.

"Hello?" she called again. "Is anyone home?"

When no one answered, she left the door standing wide open behind her while she ran back down the steps to her car.

With quick efficiency, she transferred the roasting pan, pies and bowls from her trunk to the kitchen.

By five o'clock, she had finished setting the table and she sank into the comfortable rocker and prepared to wait for Lucas.

She didn't have long to wait. It was only ten after five when the two pickups once again raced across the flat, disappeared into the coulee and climbed back on top before approaching the house.

Lucas recognized the red sports car parked in front of the house and frowned. *What's she doing here? It isn't seven o'clock yet.* He'd caught himself checking his watch too many times throughout the day, mentally counting off the hours until nighttime came and with it, the teacher.

"Well, I'll be damned. Ain't that Jennifer Mc-Cleary's car?" Murphy asked. He leaned forward in the seat, squinting to stare out the windshield. "Yep, sure is." He turned to cock an inquisitive shaggy eyebrow at Lucas. "I thought she wasn't goin' to be here until six-thirty or seven?"

Lucas shrugged. "That's what she told me."

"Hmm." Murphy's shrewd gaze searched Lucas's impassive features before he settled back against the seat. "Well, it'll be nice to see her. Sure is pretty, ain't she?"

Lucas grunted a noncommittal reply and ignored Murphy's knowing chuckle as he braked next to the small red car. He shoved open the truck door and stepped out, busying himself with letting down the tailgate and dragging out several small engine parts while Murphy walked to the house.

Josh's pickup pulled up beside him and Trey jumped out of the bed.

"Do you want me to take those over to the shop, Lucas?" Trey said.

"No, I've got them, go on in the house and help Murphy get dinner ready."

"Okay, boss."

The kid turned and limped tiredly toward the gate and the house. Lucas's gaze followed him only as far as the porch, where Jennifer was exchanging hellos with the other men. Her gaze went past them to meet his and he stared at her for a moment before turning his back and stalking off toward the machine shop with the greasy pump parts.

Jennifer couldn't read Lucas's expression, but the set of his broad shoulders didn't bode well. *Oh, well,* she thought fatalistically. *What can he do—shoot me?*

"Hey, Miss McCleary," Trey's voice interrupted her thoughts. "You're here early."

"Yes, I am," she answered easily, smiling. He was wearing a battered cowboy hat and the brim was tugged down over his forehead in a fair imitation of Lucas. "And so are you."

"Lucas let us quit earlier tonight," he said, shoving his hands into his back pockets.

"Well, time's awastin'," Murphy interjected. "we'd better get dinner on the table so you two can get at your studyin'."

"About dinner," Jennifer began, but she was speaking to broad backs as the three men followed Murphy through the front door and down the hall.

"Geez, what smells so good?" Charlie said.

"Smells just like my mama's roast beef," Murphy commented. He stepped into the kitchen and stopped abruptly.

Charlie walked straight into Murphy and jostled him aside. "What the hell are you doin', Murph?" he growled. He stepped around Murphy's still form and halted as if poleaxed.

"What's going on with you two?" Josh's deep bass voice rang with irritation and he pushed past Charlie and was halfway to the coffeemaker before he stopped in midstride.

Trey peered around Charlie and stared with confusion at the table, already set with plates, glasses and silverware, and at the countertop and stove, piled with bowls and pans.

Behind her, Jennifer heard the screen door squeak open, then softly close. *Oh, great.* She squeezed her eyes shut for a brief moment. *Lucas is here.* She opened her eyes. She knew he was behind her; some sixth sense, like radar, seemed to react whenever he was nearby and little sensors sent alert signals skittering along her nerves.

"I brought dinner," Jennifer said, speaking to their still backs. Behind her, the heat from Lucas's body reached her across the short space that separated them and tiny goose bumps sprang to life on her bare arms. In front of her, four pairs of stunned male eyes were turned on her. "I was coming out here anyway, and I love to cook, so I thought, why not bring you dinner, since you don't have a lot of time to prepare it yourselves, and..." *You're babbling, Jennifer,* she thought. *Shut up.* "I hope you don't mind."

"Mind?" Murphy's chortle of glee broke the brief silence. "If this tastes half as good as it smells, I'm liable to go down on my knees and beg you to marry me!"

"You're gonna have to stand in line." A rare smile creased Charlie's weather-beaten face and his faded blue eyes twinkled.

Jennifer smiled weakly at the four. Murphy's, Charlie's, Trey's and even Josh's face held matching grins of delight. *Four down, one to go.* She turned slowly and looked up at Lucas.

His blue gaze flicked over the expressions on the faces of the men in the kitchen before returning to fasten on Jennifer's. She felt a jolt of electrical awareness and struggled to keep her features calm and impassive.

Lucas was silent. The teacher met his look with surface calmness but a flicker of uneasiness underlay her waiting expression. He didn't want her doing nice things for him, didn't want her to be anything more than the kid's teacher. He damn sure didn't want to know that she cared enough to go out of her way to make them a hot meal. On the other hand, he'd have to be stone crazy to tell her to pack up her stuff and go home. The food smelled too good and he was too hungry.

"Whatever you brought, it sure smells better than Murphy's stew," he said.

His words released the five waiting people from their frozen tableau and Josh moved on toward the coffeemaker, while the other three lined up in front of the sink to wash.

Jennifer knew that Lucas's brief smile hadn't touched the frosty reserve in his eyes, but she was grateful for the reprieve.

The men washed quickly, and by the time Jennifer transferred the roast onto a platter and mounded the vegetables on another, they were helping her. Charlie took the platter of potatoes, glazed carrots and celery and headed for the table, while Murphy wielded a lethal-looking knife on the roast beef. Trey pulled open the refrigerator door.

Finally, everything was set out. Behind Jennifer, Lucas held her chair. She sank into it and the men quickly seated themselves. Fortunately for Jennifer's peace of mind, Lucas took a seat at the head of the table, with Trey on his left between them.

Jennifer watched in amazement as the five men applied themselves to the meal with a concentration broken only by an occasional compliment to the cook. The food disappeared with a speed that was phenomenal.

When the platters were nearly empty, Jennifer broke the silence.

"I hope you all left room for dessert."

Josh's normally brooding features lit with anticipation. "Dessert? What is it?"

"Pie—I hope you like apple."

"It's my favorite." Josh shoved back his chair and carried his plate to the sink.

Jennifer was struck speechless by the smile he gave her. Like Lucas, the grin turned his face from brooding good looks to handsomeness. She would have sworn after her first encounter with Lucas's brother that Josh hated women, or that maybe there was something about her personally that he didn't like. Now she wondered fleetingly if some tragedy had caused his silent, unapproachable demeanor.

There was only half a pie left of the three Jennifer had brought by the time the men pushed back from the table.

"We'll clean the kitchen," Lucas said, standing and carrying his empty plate to the sink. "You two go on into the living room and get started."

"All right," Jennifer responded.

She moved to push back her chair and Charlie quickly helped her, waiting with old-fashioned courtesy.

"Thank you, Charlie." She smiled up at him and he nodded at her.

"You're welcome," he said politely and waited for her to step away before he slid the chair back.

Jennifer turned and found Trey watching Charlie with thoughtful speculation. Then he glanced at her and caught her watching him and his face instantly smoothed, his eyes faintly challenging.

Trey was an intelligent young man. He'd quickly copied the actions of older, less desirable companions in the past. She hoped that he would just as easily pick up the courteous manners she'd been treated to from Charlie, Murphy and Lucas. "Are you ready, Trey?" Jennifer asked.

"Yes, ma'am," Trey said and followed her into the living room.

It was nearly eight-thirty before Jennifer closed her textbook and looked at Trey.

"I think that should do it for tonight, Trey, although we may need to go over adverbial phrases and participles again next time."

"All right." Trey stretched and yawned. "Do I have to read more of *Walden* this week?"

"Yes, I'm afraid so." Jennifer smiled at him. "Are you enjoying it?"

"You know," Trey admitted reluctantly, "I don't hate it nearly as much as I thought I would."

"Good." Jennifer decided to take his backhanded acceptance at face value and not push for more. "Read the next five pages, and the next time we meet, we'll discuss the relevancy of Thoreau's philosophy to today's environmental concerns."

Trey rolled his eyes and groaned. "Yes, ma'am."

Jennifer chuckled and answered his good-night as he ambled to the door. *Not a bad imitation of Lucas's walk,* she thought with a smile. *I wonder if he knows he's copying Lucas? First the hat, now the walk.*

She wondered if Lucas knew that Trey was showing all the signs of hero worship. If he did, how did he feel about it? He'd been so adamant about not "playing daddy'' that she was unsure how he would react to Trey's echoing his mannerisms.

She collected her books and purse and left the quiet house. The screen door squeaked as she pushed it open and walked out onto the porch.

"If you think you have to cook for us because I hired Trey and let you use my house to tutor him, you're wrong."

Lucas's deep voice startled her and she halted abruptly at the top of the porch steps. He was leaning against a porch post, arms folded across his chest, watching her. For a moment, she stared back, willing her racing heartbeat to slow down.

"I know I don't *have* to cook for you, Mr. Hightower, I wanted to. I like to cook, and I have free time now that school's out for the summer. Besides, I have to drive out here, anyway." She shrugged dismissively. "It's no big deal. If you're uncomfortable with my cooking for you, then let me do it for Trey's sake. He's still growing, and he needs hot meals in addition to the fresh air and work this summer."

"He gets hot meals," Lucas said through his teeth.

"I know," Jennifer said quickly. "I wasn't criticizing—it's just that whether you believe it or not, I'm convinced that you're giving Trey a chance at a better life this summer. I'd like to do my part, and cooking is such a small thing for me to do."

Lucas stared at her. The sun had set, but dusk was still in the offing, and the hazy, golden glow caught in her hair, striking red and gold sparks. He didn't want her on his ranch and in his house, even for the short time she spent teaching Trey every other night. He damn sure didn't want her here cooking dinner, standing on the porch waiting for him when he came home. He had a gut feeling that it would be all too easy to get accustomed to seeing her there, and all too hard to get over the loss when the summer was gone.

Still, her eyes looked at him with pleading and he couldn't tell her no.

"All right, dammit," he growled. He stalked toward her and she gave ground a step before she visibly stopped herself from retreating. "You can play house if you want to and pretend you're the kid's mommy."

His long strides carried him past her and down the steps. He was halfway to the yard gate when he spun and looked back at her.

Jennifer's breath caught in her throat. *Oh, no. He's going to change his mind.*

Chapter Five

"It was real nice of you to bring us dinner." The words were pulled from Lucas with gruff, reluctant honesty. "I can't remember when I've enjoyed a meal more." The hard planes of his face softened and the corners of his mouth twitched in an almost-smile. "And I've never had apple pie that was better. Thank you."

"You're welcome," Jennifer said gravely.

"Good night," he said abruptly before he turned and stalked off toward the machine shop.

"Good night," Jennifer said to his swiftly departing back. She doubted he heard her, for his long strides never hesitated. She watched until he disappeared through the wide doors of the wooden building.

His apology was obviously sincere, yet he'd been so clearly reluctant to give it that Jennifer didn't know whether she wanted to hug him or slug him.

Shaking her head, she decided to do neither. *Although, if I had to choose,* she reflected, *I'm not sure which would be more dangerous.*

Two nights later, Jennifer made fried chicken. Murphy and Charlie both begged her to marry them. Josh smiled at her again and Trey ate so much that Jennifer wondered privately if he'd explode.

Lucas thanked her briefly, but Jennifer noticed that he ate as much as the other four.

On Monday night, Lucas wasn't even surprised to see the teacher's little red sports car parked in front of his house.

"You know," Murphy drawled as Lucas braked to a halt beside the car, "it's gettin' to be a real pleasure to come home on the nights that Jennifer's here."

"Mmm," Lucas grunted.

"You don't think so?" Murphy looked sideways at him.

"I didn't say that." Lucas refused to be drawn into an argument. He also refused to admit that being met with the sight of Jennifer McCleary's curvy body waiting on his porch made him hungry for more than the mouth-watering food she brought with her. Tonight she was wearing a sleeveless white top, her legs tanned and bare beneath blue shorts, her hair caught up in a ponytail. "I'll tell you what I do think—she's a damn good cook."

Murphy's laughter was a short bark of sound. "You got that right, and she's a fine-lookin' woman, too. But I suppose you haven't noticed that, have you?"

Lucas didn't answer. He ignored the older man's knowing chuckle, shoved open the truck door and stepped out.

On the porch, Beastie relaxed his stiff stance at Jennifer's side and barked a welcome. His tail wagged eagerly and with it, his whole back half swaggered back and forth.

"Hey, Jennifer," Murphy called. "Is that a dog or a pony?"

"Hi, Murphy." Jennifer laughed at the barely concealed amazement on the older man's face. "He's a dog—a Labrador."

Charlie stepped up on the porch beside her and cocked his head, sniffing the air. "Smells good, what did you make us this time?"

"Spaghetti with meatballs. I hope you like Italian food?"

"Love it," he said promptly. He switched his attention to Beastie. "That's the biggest dog I've ever seen."

"He is a little large, isn't he?" Jennifer looked down and smoothed a calming palm over Beastie's head. "But he's friendly—hold out your hand."

Charlie complied and Beastie sniffed suspiciously before giving the man's palm a quick lick of approval.

Murphy, Josh, Trey and Lucas tramped up the steps and onto the porch behind Charlie. All four men eyed the huge dog with interest.

"You'd better all say hello and get his stamp of approval," Lucas said dryly. "Otherwise, he might not let us in the house."

Jennifer held the dog's collar while Murphy, Josh and Trey took turns holding out their hands to let Beastie sniff.

"I know I should have asked you before bringing him out here with me," Jennifer apologized to Lucas. "But he hates being left alone at the house in town. The last time I was out here, he knocked over the garbage can and scattered the trash all over my kitchen floor."

Just then, Charlie disappeared inside, followed by Murphy, Josh and Trey, leaving Jennifer alone on the porch with Lucas and Beastie.

"As long as he doesn't chase the horses and cattle, I don't care."

His hand dropped to the dog's head and he smoothed the soft fur. Beastie's eyes half closed as he luxuriated under the affectionate strokes; Jennifer stared at Lucas's hand and tried to ignore the warm heat that moved slowly through her veins. Beastie clearly liked Lucas, and more than liked the stroke of his fingers. Jennifer couldn't help wondering if he touched a woman with that same slow, thorough enjoyment. She struggled to remember his last words.

"That, uh, that's good. I'm sure he won't bother the horses, or the cattle."

She turned abruptly and caught the handle of the screen door.

"Wait." Lucas reached out and grabbed her arm just above the elbow. The feel of her smooth, soft, warm skin under his work-roughened hand startled him and he yanked his fingers away from her.

Jennifer went perfectly still, her fingers freezing over the door handle, before she turned and looked over her shoulder at him. His face reflected the same wary awareness that gripped her.

"If you're bound and determined to cook for us, I'll buy the food," he said gruffly. "There's a freezer on the back porch filled with meat, and the pantry is already well stocked, but if there's anything you need that isn't here, charge it to my account at the grocery store in town."

"All right." The heated tension that sprang to life with the brief grip of his hand on her arm disappeared, submerged beneath relief. She'd held her breath each evening that she'd spent at the Lazy H, waiting and wondering if and when Lucas would order her to stop using his kitchen. "Does this mean that you don't mind my making dinner?"

Lucas's gaze drifted over the smile that lit her vivid features, and felt his mouth lift in an answering, reluctant curve. "A man would be a complete fool not to appreciate the kind of meals you've been giving us."

"I never thought you were a fool, Mr. Hightower," she said, her eyes twinkling. She was so relieved that he was willing to give in and let her cook for Trey and the rest of the men, she forgot her determination to keep a cool reserve between them. "Stubborn, yes— but a fool? No. Definitely not."

"Hmm," Lucas grunted, eyeing her relaxed, glowing features. "I guess I can live with being called stubborn. But I'm damn sick of being called Mr.

Hightower,'' he added with irritation. "My name's Lucas.''

"I know your name." Jennifer's voice cooled, one pale eyebrow lifting in a faintly arrogant arc. "And I assume you're well aware that my name is Jennifer—not 'Teacher.'''

"I know." Lucas half glared at her, but amusement underlay his deep tones. "You've got a smart mouth—Jennifer," he said dryly.

"So I've been told—Lucas."

She turned and pulled open the door. Lucas watched her walk through the opening before he followed her, his gaze fastened on the sway of her hips as she walked down the hall. He sighed inwardly. She was definitely trouble. Unfortunately, telling himself that she was off-limits didn't seem to have any effect—his hormones were ignoring his common sense.

She was at the stove, bent over to peer into the oven when he entered the kitchen, and after one quick glance, Lucas forced his eyes away from the long, tanned curve of her legs, bare beneath the hem of blue shorts. He stalked to the sink.

Behind him, Lucas heard the oven door close and the smell of hot French bread and garlic butter filled the kitchen. He grabbed the towel and dried his hands, hoping to God his face didn't betray his thoughts about her legs.

As usual, the men applied themselves to their meal with single-minded absorption, the silence broken only by occasional requests to pass the salt, pepper, spaghetti or salad. It wasn't until second helpings had nearly disappeared from their plates that Murphy spoke.

"I ran into Zach Colby in town today, Josh. He asked me whether we're interested in playing poker on Saturday night." Murphy winked at Trey. "I only sit in to keep an eye on the boys." Both Josh and Lucas snorted, but Murphy ignored them. "They came to the Lazy H when Lucas was about your age and I've been tryin' to keep them out of trouble ever since."

"Yeah, right," Josh drawled. "Who was it that won my last fifty dollars playing poker last night?"

"Why, me, of course," Murphy answered, his face all innocence and virtuous dignity. "And let that be a lesson, Joshua, you can't play poker worth a damn."

"Hah." Josh rolled his eyes and leaned across the table toward Trey. "Don't ever play poker with this old buzzard, Trey, he cheats."

"I do not cheat." Murphy was indignant. "I'm just a little creative."

A roar of laughter erupted from everyone at the table, except Trey and Jennifer.

"You're creative, all right." Lucas chuckled, his eyes dancing. "Josh is right, Trey, never bet money when you're playing poker with a man as *creative* as Murphy."

"Now don't be bad-mouthin' me to the boy, Lucas," Murphy objected.

"I'm not bad-mouthing you, Murphy, I'm just telling Trey the truth."

Trey's head moved back and forth like that of a spectator at a tennis match, Jennifer thought. Murphy was growing heated, while Lucas remained calm and reasonable. Their banter was clearly grounded in a deep affection, and they had just as clearly had this particular argument before.

"You young whippersnappers think you know everything," Murphy growled in disgust.

Beside her, Trey chuckled, a deep sound of amusement. Startled, Jennifer glanced at him—it was the first time she'd heard the teenager laugh, really laugh. The wary, hard indifference that usually cloaked his features was gone. He was actually smiling.

Jennifer smiled back at him, and her gaze traveled past him to Lucas. For one brief, stunning moment, he stared at Trey with an arrested expression that held raw, naked pain.

Jennifer knew from Mrs. Fitch that there were unresolved issues between Lucas and Trey's mother, but what could Trey have done to cause the raw pain that tore apart Lucas Hightower's hard, uncompromising composure? For one brief, telling moment, she'd glimpsed a depth of torment that hinted at an open wound.

Lucas drained his coffee in one gulp and pushed back his chair to stand.

"I'm going to check on Maggie and the colt before I turn on that damn computer," he said abruptly. He knew Murphy would stay and help Trey and Jennifer clean up and knew that he should have stayed, too. But he could feel the walls closing in around him; he had to get out of the house and away from Trey.

He'd been looking at Murphy when Trey laughed. For one brief, shining moment, he'd believed, really believed, that when he turned his head, he'd see Clay's laughing face. But it was Trey, not his father, who sat at the dinner table. The trusting expression on the teenager's face had reminded Lucas so forcibly of Clay's that it was a blow. Guilt, desolation and grief had knifed through him and he'd nearly doubled over from the avalanche of pain.

He couldn't forgive himself for the events of the tragic night that had caused Trey to grow up without a father. It didn't matter that he'd gone to the still-grieving Suzie after Trey was born and offered to help raise the boy; he'd never blamed her for refusing him. Still, her words had cut to the bone when she demanded that he leave her house and stay away from her and Trey. She'd been right; he wasn't anybody's idea of father material. She couldn't, and shouldn't, have trusted him to share in the care of Clay's only son. If he'd only handled the events of that fateful night with more wisdom, Clay would have been alive to raise Trey. With Clay for a father, laughter and trust would have been second nature to the boy, just as it had been for his father.

It had been all he could do to answer Murphy and get out of the house without lashing out.

He stepped into the shadowy interior of the barn and walked down the wide aisle separating the stalls. Maggie heard him coming and dropped her muzzle over the top railing of her stall; her ears pricked forward alertly and she nickered a welcome.

Lucas scratched her ears and smoothed a hand down her soft nose, before she butted him gently with her head and nuzzled his shirt pocket.

"Damn," he said. "I forgot."

Jennifer's sandals moved almost noiselessly over the straw-strewn concrete floor, but Lucas heard her nevertheless and he looked up, his head lifting away from the mare as he watched her approach.

"Hi." Her nerves coiled tighter, jumping under his silence and steady stare. "Murphy asked me to bring you these." She held out the carrots and his gaze switched from her face to the carrots before returning. "For the horse," she added, gesturing with the handful of leafy-topped carrots toward Maggie.

The mare stretched toward the swiftly moving carrot tops and missed. She nickered in annoyance and nudged Lucas's chest with her muzzle.

"Hey," Lucas said, pushing the horse's nose back with one hand, "cut that out." He glanced at Jennifer and took the carrots from her outstretched hand. "Thanks."

"No problem." Jennifer caught a glimpse of the dark turmoil in his eyes before he turned to the mare. His profile was clear-cut and immovable, his lips set in a hard line.

She peered around the man and horse, searching the stall. "Where's her baby?" Beyond the bulk of his mother, the colt peeked out at her. "Oh, isn't he cute!"

Jennifer stepped around Lucas to lean against the gate for a closer look. The little colt stared back at her, his eyes liquid brown and curious in a face that was coal black with only a white star to relieve the darkness. He grew restive under her stare and left his mother's side, his long legs carrying him in sudden starts and stops around the perimeter of the big box stall.

Jennifer laughed in delight, her gaze flying to Lucas. "He's wonderful!"

"He should be," Lucas said dryly. When she smiled, her whole face lit up like sunshine. The cold, tight ball of grief and regret eased and began to loosen inside his chest. He wanted to wrap his arms around her and press her close, ached to bury his face in the fiery heat of her hair and absorb all the warmth and bright energy she exuded. Maybe then, the frozen wasteland within him would melt and give way to something other than pain from unhealed wounds.

Or maybe all that warm care and comfort he'd seen her offer to Trey would only rip away the layers of protection and leave him open, raw and bleeding. He'd never met a woman like Jennifer McCleary before, and he didn't trust his gut-deep, instinctive compulsion to reach out for her.

He tore his gaze away from her and stared at the foal while he struggled to remember their conversation. "Zach Colby charged me an arm and a leg for his stud," he said finally.

Jennifer glanced at Maggie's dark bay color and then at the night-black colt. "Does he look like his father?"

"You mean the color?" Lucas waited for Jennifer's nod. The movement set the soft wisps of silky hair that framed her face moving softly against her skin. He clenched his fingers over the mare's rough mane to quell the urge to touch Jennifer. "Yeah, his daddy is black with a white star on his forehead, just like this colt, except Colby's stud has three white socks."

Maggie chose that moment to nudge Lucas again and he turned back to her. "Okay, okay," he murmured. "You're getting demanding, Maggie."

Jennifer watched him feed one of the carrots to the horse. The carrot disappeared with amazing swiftness, the mare crunching loudly as her strong jaws ground up the treat. The sound was the only interruption in the quiet of the barn.

"Actually," Jennifer confided, resting her forearms on the top of the gate and glancing sideways at him, "Murphy didn't ask me to bring the carrots for Maggie—I volunteered."

"Really?" Lucas swept an assessing glance over her before returning to Maggie. "Something tells me you weren't just being helpful."

Jennifer shrugged. "Not entirely. I wanted to talk to you about what happened at dinner. Is Trey in trouble—has he done something to upset you?"

He stiffened and a muscle jumped in his jaw. "What makes you think he upset me?"

"It's obvious that something upset you. One minute you and Murphy were having a conversation and the next minute you were gone."

"And you leaped to the conclusion that my leaving had something to do with Trey?"

"I saw you look at him, Lucas." She was determined not to let him avoid this discussion. "You were obviously upset."

Lucas flicked her an unreadable glance. "If I was, it has nothing to do with you."

"Yes, it does," she said determinedly. "Everything that concerns Trey concerns me. If he's done something wrong, he deserves to know what it is so that he can rectify it."

"He hasn't done anything."

"Lucas, stop being so stubborn." Exasperation crept into her tone.

"The kid hasn't done a damn thing except be born," he snarled. "And there isn't anything he can do about that."

"I don't understand. You're angry with him because he was born?"

"No."

Frustrated, Jennifer frowned at him. "Lucas, you're not making sense. I can't help if you won't talk to me."

"You can't help." His words were bleak, carrying a flat rejection.

"How do you know? You could at least let me try."

"It wouldn't matter how hard you tried, some things in life are beyond help. There's no fixing what's been broken."

"Does this have anything to do with Trey's parents? With his father?"

Lucas's features went even harder, his eyes hot with anger.

"What do you know about his father?" he demanded roughly.

"Only what Mrs. Fitch told me, that you and Clay Webber were best friends, that you traveled the rodeo circuit after high school and that Suzie joined you to marry Clay. And that a year later, Clay died in an accident."

Lucas knew a fierce surge of relief that Annabel Fitch had been the one to tell the teacher about Clay and Suzie. He'd overheard at least a dozen versions of the story through the years. They ran the gamut from outrageous to impossible, and none of them had treated him well.

He was silent, staring unseeingly at the mare and her colt. Jennifer waited patiently, but he didn't speak.

"Was she wrong?" she asked finally.

"No." Lucas's voice was rusty, the words rasped over his throat. "No, she wasn't wrong. Clay was my best friend," he said reluctantly, the words pulled from him. "Trey looks a lot like him, even sounds like him when he talks, and when he laughs... Tonight it just caught me by surprise, that's all."

"Oh." Jennifer was silent for a moment, soberly considering the set lines of his face. "That's what you meant when you said that he couldn't help being born? That he looks like his dad and sometimes the resemblance is... painful?"

"Yeah."

The short, reluctant acknowledgment carried a wealth of meaning. Jennifer guessed that Lucas wasn't a man who admitted emotions easily. Impulsively, she laid a hand on his forearm.

"I'm sorry, Lucas, I didn't realize when I asked you to hire Trey for the summer that it would be so difficult."

Lucas felt the warm touch of her slim fingers against his bare arm like a brand. Smooth and slender, they lay gently against the darker skin of his arm. Watching her with Trey, he'd wondered how it would feel to have her warm compassion centered on him. Now he knew, and the need to press her close and take what she offered was almost overwhelming.

He forced himself to relax, unclenching taut muscles. Fortunately, Maggie chose that moment to nudge him again, exhaling noisily.

"Uh-oh." Lucas smoothed a palm down the mare's nose and glanced at Jennifer. "I think she's tired of waiting for the rest of her treat. Want to feed her?"

"Uh, well . . ." Jennifer's gaze flicked from Maggie's teeth to Lucas. The hard planes of his face were less tense, his muscular body more relaxed as he leaned against the stall gate. She looked at the mare again, studying the ground pieces of carrot that escaped her muzzle to sprinkle the straw beneath her front hooves. "I don't know—I'm not sure I wouldn't lose a few fingers," she said.

Lucas chuckled. Jennifer's expressive face held equal parts fascination and apprehension. "Maggie won't eat your fingers—she likes carrots a lot better than humans. Come on, she won't bite you."

Jennifer stepped closer and took the carrot, holding it toward the horse at arm's length. The mare stretched out her neck, her lips curling back from strong, yellow teeth as she bit a good three inches off the end of the carrot.

"Yikes." Jennifer transferred the carrot to the tips of her fingers and looked over her shoulder at Lucas. "Are you sure she won't bite me?"

"I'm sure." Lucas's chest brushed against her shoulders as he reached around her and took the carrot from her hands.

Jennifer was surrounded by warm, strong male. Her shoulder blades pressed lightly against Lucas's chest, his arms wrapping her in their circle, and powerful muscles flexed with easy strength as he snapped the remaining carrot into two pieces.

"Hold out your hand, palm up." She obeyed and he dropped one of the sections on her open hand. "Keep your palm flat—don't curl it up—and she'll take it off your palm."

He stepped back, breaking the contact of body against body, and Jennifer drew in a deep breath. Her face felt flushed and heated, her heartbeat raced, and for a moment, she stared stupidly at the carrot in her hand, trying to remember what she was supposed to do with it.

Just then, Maggie reached out and lipped the last chunk of carrot from her palm, and Jennifer jumped in surprise. Her quick, startled step bumped her into Lucas and his hands closed over the curve of her shoulders to hold her against him. The contact with his hard, muscled bulk sent heat lightning shuddering through her and she twisted out of his grasp, turning to face him.

Lucas stared down into her apprehensive face. The urge to reach out and pull her against him was strong, especially when the flush on her face and the surprised awareness in her expression told him that she wasn't unaffected by his touch. The strength of his own need, reflected in the unguarded gaze turned up to his, shocked him.

"I'd better get back to the house," Jennifer said, determinedly casual. "Trey's probably waiting for me."

"Yeah." Lucas's voice was gravelly with the effort it took to speak. "I'm sure he is."

Nerves on edge, she backed away from him several steps before she turned and hurried down the broad aisle. She stepped into the waning sunshine and drew a deep breath into starved lungs, only then realizing that she'd been barely breathing since their bodies had touched in the barn.

She walked quickly across the yard, up the porch steps and into the house. Behind her, a pickup engine growled into life and she glanced out the screen door just in time to see Lucas's truck leaving.

She guessed he wasn't going to use the computer tonight, after all.

The wired tension drained out of her, leaving her feeling curiously flat. Shaken by her inability to remain unaffected by the big rancher, she turned on her heel and headed for the kitchen.

Lucas was avoiding her.

She told herself she should be relieved. The less she saw of him, the easier it would be to control her unwanted response to him. *And it is unwanted,* she told herself firmly.

So she cooperated. She treated him with polite distance, avoided eye contact and pretended not to notice when he left the kitchen immediately after dessert. When she stepped out on the front porch after tutoring Trey, she no longer found him leaning against the railing, looking out into the dark night.

She told herself she didn't miss him. But her conscience scoffed at her.

One week slipped into two, and then three. Jennifer was beginning to think that she and Lucas were going to spend the summer successfully sidestepping each other, when Trey asked her to teach him how to use her computer.

"I'd be delighted to teach you the basics, Trey." She beamed at him with approval. "I didn't know you were interested in computers."

He shrugged and tried to look nonchalant. "I'm interested in everything about ranching, and Murphy says that using a computer to keep track of the business end of running a ranch is something a man has to know."

"I see." Jennifer had a strong suspicion that Trey's interest in computers had more to do with watching Lucas disappear into the office every evening than Murphy's opinion on the subject. "I suppose that I could bring my laptop computer with me to our study sessions, but I'm not sure that we can fit another subject into our schedule, Trey."

"Couldn't we drop something we're already doing and study computers instead?" he asked hopefully.

"I don't think so, Trey. We have a lot to cover this summer, and although you're making great progress, we're not at a point where you're ready to drop any of the subjects you're studying."

Trey's shoulders slumped in dejection. "So I guess there's no chance."

"There is one possibility," Jennifer said slowly. "We could expand our sessions to another night or two more every week."

Trey brightened and sat forward in his chair. "Yeah? You'd be willing to do that for me?"

"Yes—if you're willing to give up more of your free time."

"Absolutely," he answered, giving her a smile free of dark shadows.

"I'll have to talk to Lucas," she warned. "And he may not want to give up his living room for another night or two every week."

"Oh, he won't mind," Trey said confidently.

Jennifer wasn't so sure.

She was even less sure later that evening. Trey had said good-night and left for the bunkhouse and she stood alone in the quiet living room, gathering her courage to talk to Lucas.

The door to the office, just to the right of the stairwell, was closed, but a splinter of light beneath it told her that Lucas was still inside. She raised her hand and knocked on the white-enameled panel.

"Come in."

Lucas's deep voice sounded distracted. Jennifer took a deep breath and pushed the door inward.

He looked up from the open file on his lap and went perfectly still, his eyes focusing on Jennifer's slim figure. His lightning glance flicked from her crown to her feet and back up again, taking in the feminine curves covered in a loose sundress. The dress had tiny sleeves, a modest, scooped neckline and a dozen or more little blue buttons that drew a line between the swell of her breasts and down the front of her body to below her knees; the soft material, with dark blue flowers scattered over a white background, skimmed her curves and fell to midcalf.

The dress wasn't tight, and it was too modest to be blatantly sexy, but Lucas had a swift mental image of slowly slipping free every one of those buttons. He forced himself to stop thinking about what she might be wearing under that dress with its blue flowers and fastened his gaze above her chin.

"Are you and Trey finished for the night?" he asked finally.

Jennifer pushed a hand through her hair and shifted it back over her shoulder. Lucas sat with his boot-shod feet crossed at the ankle and propped on the edge of the battered wooden desk. His long legs were encased in his usual faded blue jeans.

The air fairly crackled between them, the force of his personality reaching out across the room and shrinking the space that separated them. The knowledge that avoiding him hadn't lessened his attraction was dismaying.

"Yes, we've finished." She stepped farther into the room and gestured toward the file. "I need to talk to you about Trey, but I can wait until later if this is a bad time."

Lucas glanced down at the open file and flipped it shut, tossing it on top of the desk. "No, this is as good a time as any. What's up?"

Jennifer walked toward him, hesitated and detoured to take a seat on a sturdy, worn leather sofa. She fiddled with her skirt, smoothing it over her knees before looking up at him.

"Is there some problem with Trey?" he prompted, his voice deeper, huskier than before.

"It isn't exactly a problem, at least not for Trey," she said. "But it may be a problem for you."

One dark eyebrow rose skeptically. "For me? Why? What's he done?"

"It's not what he's done, it's what he wants to do," she explained. "He wants to learn computer skills."

Lucas glanced away from her and at the computer screen a foot away from his boots atop the desk. "And he wants to use mine? I'm not sure if—"

"No," she interrupted. "He doesn't need to use your computer—I have a laptop we can use—but our schedule is full. I can't possibly add another class to our regular lessons without keeping him up until after eleven, and that wouldn't allow him enough hours of sleep." She gestured helplessly, her hands lifting in a graceful movement before falling back to her lap. "I'm already concerned that he may need more rest than he's getting."

"So what are you suggesting?" His voice was perfectly even, with no inflection.

"I'm suggesting that I add another evening or two to Trey's tutoring schedule. I know that it's a terrible imposition, Lucas, but Trey seems genuinely interested in learning to use a computer and it's a skill that will be immensely helpful in college."

"College?" Lucas eyed her. "I thought you were worried about him making it through high school?"

She shrugged impatiently. "I was—I am. But Trey is one of the brightest students I've ever had. There isn't any reason he can't go to college, given enough encouragement. He's made amazing progress this summer, and I want that to continue. That's why it's so important that he be able to explore other academic interests and why I'd like to expand his tutoring schedule."

Lucas stared at her assessingly. "You're amazing, Teacher. I've never known a woman who was as bulldog determined to help a kid that's not even hers."

"I'm a teacher," she said. Her spine stiffened and she stared reprovingly at his sprawled figure. "Trey is a student with great potential and he doesn't seem to have a parent willing to help him. I can't just ignore all the promise I see in him."

Her voice was sharp and Lucas's hard mouth lifted in a half smile. "A lot of people in town would tell you that he has promise, all right, but I don't think their definition of his potential is the same as yours."

"Then they don't know him the way I do," she said tightly.

"You've only been in town a few months," he said. "What makes you see him clearer than anyone else?"

"Teaching teenagers gives you a different perspective," she replied. "Besides, I'm not the only one who sees a bright future for Trey. Annabel Fitch agrees with me."

"Yeah, well..." Lucas rubbed the back of his neck and avoided her gaze. "Annabel Fitch tends to see the good in everybody, whether it's there or not."

Jennifer was silent, watching him. Did he think Annabel had been wrong to believe in him all those years ago? He exuded such strength and quiet confidence that it seemed impossible he might question his own worth.

"In the short time since I met her," she commented thoughtfully, "I haven't known her to be wrong."

"Mmm." Lucas's reply was noncommittal. He combed his fingers through the ruffled thickness of his hair. "When do you want to tutor Trey in computers?"

"If you agree, I can expand our evening sessions to Monday through Friday. That will give him two hours of question-and-answer, and two hours of hands-on practice on my computer." Jennifer spoke quickly, seeing the frown that grew as he listened to her, but refusing to back down.

"Monday through Friday," he repeated slowly, his drawl more pronounced.

"I know it's asking a lot," Jennifer interjected. "You'll be giving up your living room five nights out of seven."

"Who the hell cares if I can't use the living room," he growled. "The fact is, I'm going to have a woman and a kid under my feet five nights out of the week instead of three."

"We can always move to the bunkhouse if you have guests," Jennifer offered, ignoring his black scowl.

He laughed. It was really more of a half groan, half chuckle, and Jennifer, braced for a long argument, frowned in confusion.

"The only kind of guests I'm likely to have would be more comfortable playing poker in the bunkhouse than you would be out there with your computer," he said wryly, his mouth quirking in a self-derisive smile.

Jennifer eyed him, wondering what he was thinking, but quickly gave up the attempt to find out. "Does that mean we have your permission?"

"Yeah." He swung his feet down from the desk and stood, looking at her. She automatically rose from the sofa and squared off in front of him. "If the kid has an interest in computers, teach him," he said. "Maybe he'll learn enough to do some of the book work for me—I hate the damn thing."

"I don't know if he'll become good enough to handle your work, but I'll certainly do my best to teach him all I know."

"Great."

She shifted under his gaze, glanced toward the closed door and realized that they were all alone in the quiet house.

"Well," she said brightly. "I guess I should be going—would you tell Trey that I'll be back tomorrow night?"

"Sure." He nodded, noticing the smile that flashed quickly and the glance she shot him from beneath her lashes. His body tightened at the small, revealing movements.

"Good night then."

"Good night."

She crossed quickly to the door and slipped out, closing it quietly behind her. Lucas stood immobile, staring at the panels while he listened for the squeak and soft slap of the screen door closing behind her.

"Hightower," he said with weary disgust, "you're an idiot. Five nights a week of cold showers instead of three. Why didn't you just tell her no?" He tucked the tips of his fingers in the back pockets of his jeans and shook his head at his own hopeless lack of willpower. "Because when she gets that serious, hopeful look on her face, you couldn't tell her no even if it meant prison, and you know it. Maybe I should just corner her, haul her off to the bedroom and get her out of my system."

He stared at the flickering computer screen for a long moment, picturing the possibility of Jennifer in his bed, before he gave a long, gusty sigh. "Nah." He reached out and turned off the computer. "Even if she agreed, she's the kind of woman who'd expect wedding bells and babies."

For the first time in his life, the thought of permanence in connection with a woman didn't make him shudder in revulsion. Stunned, he turned his back on the office and the possibility, and left the room for his bed.

By mid-July, Jennifer had fallen into a comfortable routine that had her driving out to the Lazy H every Monday through Friday.

Lucas continued to keep contact with her to a minimum, and guilt that he was literally forced out of his home because of her began to nag her with increasingly uncomfortable frequency.

Trey, oblivious to the currents that swirled around the two adults, thrived. He gained weight, grew taller and walked straighter, with a new self-confidence that carried over into his studies.

"Your penmanship is improving, Trey," Jennifer told him one night, glancing up at him from the sheet of English homework that lay on the table in front of her. "I can read almost every word."

Trey shifted in his chair and shrugged off the compliment. "I got tired of you asking me to translate it for you," he grumbled.

Jennifer watched the light red that brushed across his cheekbones and the brief flash of bashful pleasure that lit his eyes before he quickly wiped all expression from his face. The dark circles were nearly gone now from beneath his eyes and his smile lit his youthful face more often, lightening the world-weary, cynical set of his features.

"But you read aloud so well," she teased, smiling at the teenager.

"Yeah, right," he answered. He ducked his head and pretended to study the open textbook on the table before him.

"I'm serious, you really do." Jennifer leaned her chin on her hand and considered the top of his head. "Have you ever thought about trying out for the drama club during school?"

Trey raised his head, startled, and he fixed her with a disbelieving stare. "Are you crazy?"

"No, not at all," she assured him calmly. "I think you'd be very good."

"Sure," Trey said wryly. "I can see it now—me, dressed in tights, spouting Romeo's words to Juliet— 'Juliet, Juliet, let down your hair.'"

Jennifer burst into laughter. "That's not *Romeo and Juliet!*"

"Sure it is." Trey frowned at her. "Juliet's the one up on the balcony wearing the funny hat and Romeo's the guy down on the ground wearing sissy tights."

"Boy, have you got a garbled version of Shakespeare. How did you get *Romeo and Juliet* so mixed up with a fairy tale?"

"What fairy tale?" Trey asked suspiciously.

"Rapunzel," Jennifer answered promptly. "That's the one where the prince at the base of the tower asks her to let down her hair and he climbs up the tower to save her."

"Are you sure?"

"Positive."

"Yeah, well, I bet the prince wore sissy tights."

Out of sight and unnoticed in the kitchen, Lucas poured a fresh mug of coffee and listened to their exchange, grinning. Rapunzel? He didn't blame the kid for getting the story confused with *Romeo and Juliet*—he'd never heard of Rapunzel, either. But then, reading fairy tales to children was one of the things that mothers were supposed to do. He'd been seven years old when Monica Hightower had left her husband and two small sons for greener pastures, and even before she'd left, she'd had little interest in spending time with her children.

He leaned his hips against the counter, crossed his arms and sipped his coffee while he listened to Jennifer and Trey.

She's good with him, he thought, hearing the gentle teasing underlaid with firmness when Trey objected to a homework assignment. *Hell, who am I kidding? She's good with all of us—Trey, Murphy, Charlie—even Josh smiles more when she's around. The only one she's driving crazy is me.*

The scrape of chairs sounded in the living room as Jennifer and Trey stood and gathered up books, papers and pens, finished with their session for the evening.

Yawning, Trey tucked his books under his arm and left to find his bed, and Jennifer collected her empty coffee mug and a plate littered with the crumbs from chocolate chip cookies.

Humming softly, she walked into the kitchen and stopped dead still.

Lucas was leaning against the counter not ten feet away, staring at her.

Chapter Six

"Oh. I didn't know you were here," she managed to say. After days of exchanging polite conversation only when necessary, and with at least two other people present, it was a distinct shock to face him alone.

The bright glare of the overhead light found ebony sparks in his black hair and gleamed off skin burnished dark by sun and wind. He'd showered and changed into clean jeans and a white cotton shirt.

"I live here," Lucas commented dryly. He lifted the coffee mug to his lips and eyed her over the rim. She half frowned at him, hesitating in the doorway with a mug in one hand and an empty plate in the other. Her face was as easy to read as an open book. "Come on in, I don't bite."

Any hint of uncertainty vanished. Her spine stiffened, her chin tilted stubbornly and she shot him a look of complete irritation.

"I wasn't afraid you would," she said frostily. She marched across the kitchen, the hem of her white shorts brushing against the denim of his jeans when she halted at the sink and turned on the water with a quick twist. Water gushed into the sink, spraying small drops onto the front of her yellow cotton blouse and Lucas's sleeve.

"Sorry," she muttered, casting a quick glance at him. He didn't appear to have noticed the tiny drops that dampened his shirt; instead, his gaze was fastened on her hair. Pulled back from her face with combs, the heavy mass swung free down her back. Jennifer switched her attention to the mug and plate she was rinsing, determinedly ignoring the heat that moved into her cheeks.

She tipped the mug and plate upside down on the wooden dish drainer by the sink and caught up the towel to dry her hands. The silence stretched between them. Jennifer hung the damp towel over the rack, smoothed out nonexistent wrinkles and searched for the right words. She finally decided that the direct approach was best. "Lucas, I think we need to talk."

"Really? What about?" His deep voice was carefully neutral.

She turned to face him, shrinking the few feet separating them by another three inches. He was so close she could have touched him by taking one small step, but she refused to move away and let him know that he made her nervous.

"It's obvious that you're not comfortable having me in the house," she said. "I think we need to talk about an alternative—Trey and I could use the poker table in the bunkhouse for our lessons.''

Lucas was silent for a long moment. Not comfortable? That was far too mild a description for what had become outright torture. Everything about Jennifer McCleary turned him on, from the tilt of her stubborn chin and the riot of silky red curls, to her long, tanned legs that he ached to have wrapped around his waist. Preferably while they were both completely naked, which was happening all too often in his dreams. Unfortunately, she was clearly not the type for a short, hot affair. Even if she were, some gut-deep, primal instinct warned him to leave her alone. "It wouldn't make a damn bit of difference if you were in the house or the bunkhouse."

Jennifer flushed at the confirmation that he didn't want her on the Lazy H.

"I don't have an alternative plan," she began. "I'd be glad to tutor Trey at my home, but I don't know how I'd get him there...."

"That wouldn't make any difference, either."

His flat statement left no room for argument and Jennifer stared at him in frustration.

"Look, Lucas, I'm sorry you've taken such a dislike to me, but I haven't a clue what I've done to cause it, nor what I can do to rectify it. If there's something I can do, or should stop doing, tell me."

Lucas laughed, a reluctant, frustrated growl of male amusement.

"I don't suppose you'd consider getting naked and spending the night with me?"

Jennifer's mouth dropped open and she stared at him in shock. "That isn't funny, Lucas. I wish you'd be serious about this."

"Oh, I'm serious," he answered with self-derision. "And if I thought for one minute that you'd agree, I'd be tempted to take you to bed right now and spend the next ten hours getting you out of my system."

"Ten hours?" Jennifer echoed, grappling with the images that his words brought flashing to life in vivid Technicolor.

"At least," Lucas agreed. He skimmed over her astounded features, down her slim shape, to her feet, and back up again. "Hell," he muttered. "I don't know if ten hours would even come close. It might take longer, a lot longer."

"Longer?"

"Yeah, longer," he growled. Instead of shocking her into outrage, his blunt words had brought a heated flush to her face; fascination and curiosity lurked beneath the shock in her golden eyes. Holding her gaze trapped with his, he reached behind him to set his cup on the counter and gave in to the need to touch what had been eating holes in him since the first time he saw her. He slid his fingers into the thickness of her hair, rubbing the satiny strands between thumb and forefinger with slow, sensual pleasure. "Silk," he murmured.

Jennifer's heart beat like a wild thing, her breathing suspended at the look on Lucas's hard face. Fascination warred with yearning, but quickly faded beneath the hot need that gleamed in his eyes, shuttered behind half-lowered lashes. His free hand brushed gently, tenderly against her cheek.

"And skin like satin," he breathed with husky confirmation. Her face cupped in his palm, his thumb rubbed gently, once, twice, three times, over her lower lip.

Jennifer's lips parted, obeying the silent coaxing. Too heavy to hold open, her eyelids fell closed and above her, she heard Lucas's harsh, indrawn breath just before his mouth took hers.

The world narrowed to the slow, drugging movements of his mouth on hers. Her knees gave way and if it hadn't been for his arms tightening around her and the hard, heated length of his body that he gathered her against, Jennifer would have collapsed. She didn't give a thought to the danger; she wrapped her arms around his neck, her fingers threading into his thick hair to hold him closer, her mouth urgent under his.

Holding her was better than it was in his dreams, Lucas thought dimly. Her soft, curved shape fit neatly against his harder angles; the silky, fragrant mass of her hair brushed against his face and shoulders. Her mouth was soft, hot and eager beneath his.

Lucas groaned. He knew he had to let her go. She was even more dangerous than he'd thought and kissing her could become addictive.

But instead of releasing her, he lifted his mouth only long enough to change the angle of the kiss. *Just one more,* he told himself. *Then I'll stop.*

Long moments passed, the silence of the kitchen broken only by the soft murmurs of pleasure from deep in Jennifer's throat and muted groans from Lucas.

At last, Lucas reluctantly lifted his mouth from hers. Her soft body lay trustingly against his, her lashes lifting slowly to reveal golden eyes that were dazed with arousal. Hot blood surged through his veins and instinct bent his head toward her once more, his arms tightening to drag her closer before sanity reasserted itself.

With an effort, he forced himself to loosen his hold. Even as he watched, Jennifer's eyes were clearing, the clouds of desire giving way to alarm, only to be swiftly followed by wariness. She stiffened, pushing away from him, and he let her go, catching her waist in a gentle grip when she stumbled before her knees regained their ability to hold her.

"We've both been wondering what it would be like," he said, his voice thick with repressed, frustrated need. "Now we know."

"Yes," Jennifer murmured. "Now we know." She stared at him. How could he stop kissing her and speak rationally? Her head was still spinning, her heart shuddering in her chest, and she had to concentrate on breathing in and out.

"You might as well stick to your schedule—use the house for your lessons with Trey. Like I said, it wouldn't make a damn bit of difference if you moved to the bunkhouse."

"All right," she whispered, her throat going dry at the heat that flared in his eyes. A wry smile tilted his mouth.

"To tell you the truth, it might help if you'd try not to look so pretty. Maybe you could start wearing a bag over your head? And covering up the rest of you with gunnysacks, especially your legs."

Heat flooded Jennifer.

"I've never met a man who was quite so—forthright—about his feelings," she commented.

"I'm not going to wrap this up in pretty ribbons, Jennifer. I want you. I'd like nothing better than to spend hours somewhere with just you, me and a bed. Hell, I'd do without the bed and settle for just you and me. But I don't do happily-ever-after. If I thought you were the kind of woman to settle for a hot affair and we could both walk away with no regrets when it was over, I'd have both of us naked so fast your head would spin. But I doubt that you want that."

Silence filled the kitchen.

"If I'm wrong, all you have to do is say so."

His rough voice held all the promise of heaven and the danger of hell.

Jennifer wanted to say yes. Every aroused nerve in her body clamored for it. But somewhere deep inside her, an ingrained, instinctive sense of survival demanded to be heard.

Lucas knew the minute she made her decision. Her lashes lowered, hiding her thoughts from him, and a slight shudder shook her taut frame.

"No, you're not wrong," she said steadily, only a slight tremble betraying the strength it took to deny him. "I don't have affairs—I never have, and I don't think it would be wise to start now."

Lucas shrugged in an attempt at indifference, but his body was strung too tight to move smoothly. "It's probably for the best. This is going to be a hell of a long summer—we don't need to complicate it any more than we already have."

Jennifer nodded, forcing her eyes to meet his. "Are you sure you want me to stay on? Maybe there's some other solution to teaching Trey that we haven't thought of yet, and—"

"No," he interrupted. Even knowing that it would be torture having her near, he still couldn't bring himself to ask her to stop coming to the Lazy H. "We're adults. There's no reason why we can't deal with this."

"So we'll be…friends?" Jennifer wasn't at all sure that this was going to work.

"Sure, why not?" Lucas nearly groaned aloud at the doubtful look on her face. There was no way in hell that the two of them could be friends. Lovers, maybe, but friends? He understood and shared her doubt; still, he was damn sure that he didn't want to let her go, and friendship seemed the only road left.

"All right, if you say so." Jennifer was anything but convinced, but he seemed adamant. She realized with shock that the dusk outside the windows had given way to the blackness of night. "My goodness, look at the time!" She turned and hurried into the living room to gather up her books and purse.

Lucas didn't try to stop her; instead, he followed her to the door and said good-night. She was obviously uncomfortable. He told himself that her reaction was normal, given the circumstances. *Hell, who am I kidding?* he thought with self-derision while he watched her car toss up dust as it raced down the lane to the county road. *I haven't a clue what's normal for two people who decide to be just friends when they're so hot for each other that they'd probably set the sheets on fire.*

Shaking his head at his own idiocy, he mounted the steps to his bedroom, knowing full well that he'd sentenced himself to a sleepless night filled with dreams of Jennifer that kept him tossing, turning and twisting the sheets. Kissing her hadn't helped his condition. Now that he knew how she tasted, his dreams were bound to get even hotter and more frustrating.

Jennifer suffered from her own share of sleepless hours that night.

"Thank goodness today is Saturday," she told Beastie the next morning. She stood in the kitchen, her hair tousled, her eyelashes drooping from lack of sleep, while she waited patiently for the coffeemaker to finish brewing. She yawned and bent to scratch the big dog behind his ears. "I won't have to see Lucas until Monday night. Maybe by then, I'll be able to look at him without having X-rated thoughts."

Beastie woofed in commiseration, nudging his cold nose against her knee, bare beneath the hem of her thigh-length T-shirt.

Jennifer jumped at the unexpected, wet contact and tugged on one velvety brown ear. "Hey, you, stop that! Between Lucas and Trey, I have more than enough trouble with men. I don't need any from you."

Beastie seemed to know that she needed support, for he followed her closely all morning as she cleaned house. Unfortunately, the nonstop activity didn't keep her from thinking about Lucas. And that kiss.

Jennifer decided to eat lunch out.

It wasn't that being alone with her thoughts was driving her crazy, she told herself stoutly. Lucas Hightower wasn't the first man who'd kissed her, and he wouldn't be the last. What really bothered her was that he was the first man who she'd kissed back with mindless, driving need. He left her aching. She'd never felt that way before. And what scared her even more was that she was beginning to realize what powerful forces her passionate, vulnerable mother had struggled with. And lost.

How much like her mother was she?

It was hot. Beneath the thin leather soles of her sandals, the concrete sidewalk was searing and the sun heated the crown of her head beneath her straw hat. Luckily, it was only six short blocks to the main street of Butte Creek.

Welcome coolness hit her the moment she pushed open the glass door and stepped into the interior of Connie's Café.

"Hi, Miss McCleary."

Jennifer removed her hat and smiled at Cindy Bowers, a classmate of Trey's who had been in her third-period English Lit class. Cindy's mother owned the café and waitressing in the small family restaurant kept the teenager busy during the summer.

"Hi, Cindy, how are you?"

"Just fine. Sure is hot today, isn't it?"

"Yes," Jennifer agreed, fanning herself with her hat. "It certainly is."

Cindy tucked a plastic-covered menu under her arm, picked up a pitcher of ice water and gestured for Jennifer to follow her to the back of the café.

On the way there, Jennifer halted beside a low-backed booth. "Mrs. Fitch!" Her voice reflected the pleasure she felt at the sight of the older woman. "I didn't know you were back from Helena."

"Good afternoon, Jennifer." Annabel Fitch smiled. "You look as if this break has been good for you."

"Oh, it has," Jennifer assured her with heartfelt enthusiasm. "I can't remember when I've gotten as much rest, or as much exercise," she added with a grin. "I've been getting up at five to go jogging with Beastie."

"Oh, my goodness." Annabel laughed, the creases at the corners of her eyes deepening. "What about your evenings—are you still tutoring Trey?"

"Yes."

"And how is it going?"

"Miss McCleary?" Beyond Jennifer, Cindy shifted closer, her voice tentative as she interrupted the two women. "Your booth is ready."

"Why don't you join me, Jennifer?" Annabel suggested. "You can tell me all about Trey while you eat lunch."

"Thanks." Jennifer dropped onto the red bench and settled her hat on the seat beside her. Cindy quickly took down her order.

Annabel watched the slim girl hurry off, before turning back to Jennifer. "Not only is that girl a good student, but she's a hard worker. Her parents have done a good job. Now," she said briskly, fixing Jennifer with an intent gaze. "Tell me about Trey."

Jennifer sipped her water, wondering where to begin.

"Well," she said slowly. "He's making amazing progress in his studies and voluntarily took on extra study time to learn how to use my computer."

"Really?" Annabel's eyes lit. "That's excellent! Will he be able to continue with his class next year, or will he need to repeat classes?"

"He'll move on. As a matter of fact, I wouldn't be surprised if he gives our top students a run for their money."

"And how is he doing with the work on the Lazy H?"

"Very well. He seems to get along with the men and Lucas says he works hard and is willing to attempt any job he's assigned, which goes a long way toward making up for what he doesn't know about ranch work."

Cindy arrived with the salad and Jennifer was silent while the girl refilled their water glasses before being called away.

"He seems less hostile," Jennifer continued. "He laughs more, and as far as I know, he hasn't been in any trouble this summer."

"Has he had time?" Annabel asked dryly, sipping her own iced tea. "Or has Lucas kept him too busy and too tired for mischief?"

"Now that you mention it," Jennifer said, stabbing a forkful of lettuce, cucumber and tomato while she considered the question, "I don't remember Trey mentioning that he's been away from the Lazy H, except to ride into town with Murphy or Josh on errands." She grinned. "Maybe Trey's being so good because he hasn't had an opportunity to be anything else."

Annabel chuckled. "It's entirely possible," she agreed. "But whatever caused his good behavior, I'm glad to hear that he's accomplishing something this summer besides getting into trouble.''

"He's healthier, too," Jennifer said, crunching a bread stick. "And he's gained weight."

"Really? That surprises me. Lucas told me last summer that none of the men out there could cook worth a darn. Did he hire someone new?"

Jennifer shifted uncomfortably against the upholstered bench, crossing one bare leg across the other and fiddling with her sweat-beaded water glass.

"Actually, no." She lifted her gaze from the tabletop to Annabel's face. "I've been cooking."

Annabel blinked. "*You've* been cooking? Out at the Lazy H?"

Jennifer nodded. "Yes. Just on the nights I drive out to tutor Trey."

"And how many nights a week is that?"

"Five, at the moment. We began with only three nights a week, but since we added computer studies, we've increased the nights to five."

"I see." Annabel successfully hid a small smile of satisfaction. "That's kind of you, Jennifer. I'm sure Lucas and all of the men appreciate it."

"I started doing it for Trey." Jennifer wasn't sure why she was explaining herself to Annabel, but something about the smile in the older woman's eyes forced the words from her throat. "He was so thin. The first night I went out to the ranch, the men got home late and I was there when they made dinner—out of cans. Later, Trey told me that it was normal for them to throw together a fast meal and that Lucas would have hired a cook for the summer if he hadn't hired him. I'm really not sure why I'm doing it, Annabel." Jennifer frowned slightly. "I thought that cooking meals for them on the nights I was at the ranch was the least I could do in return for Lucas's agreeing to hire Trey for the summer."

"And when you asked Lucas if you could prepare meals, did he object?" Annabel asked.

"I didn't exactly *ask* him." Jennifer sipped her iced tea and toyed with the loose end of her braid. "I sort of just did it. When they got home from work, dinner was almost on the table."

"No kidding?" Annabel asked. "What did he do?"

"What could he do?" Jennifer asked dryly, a half smile lifting her mouth as she remembered her nervousness. "The men were starving and so was he. Nobody was going to turn down hot roast beef and potatoes—not to mention apple pie."

Annabel's eyes twinkled. "Ah, the age-old way to a man's heart—through his stomach."

"I don't want his heart," Jennifer said hastily. "I just want him to let me teach Trey and keep the boy well fed this summer. If that means that Lucas and the other men also get hot meals, then so much the better. But I'm not doing it for Lucas, only for Trey."

"That may be," Annabel commented. "But you've managed to accomplish what half the women in the county have never been able to do."

"What's that?" Jennifer asked.

"Spend time with Lucas." Annabel chuckled at Jennifer's expression. "Hasn't anyone told you that Lucas Hightower avoids women like the plague?"

"You're kidding!" Dumbfounded, Jennifer stared at her white-haired companion. "Why?"

"I think it started with his mother deserting the family when he was a child. She wasn't very maternal but at least the boys got a meal on occasion and had clean clothes while she lived with their father. After she left, they pretty much shifted for themselves. Lucas was only seven years old and Josh four. Their father was drunk most of the time so Lucas took care of his little brother. They didn't have the best of clothes and the other children, especially the girls, teased them unmercifully. During high school, before Wayne took them in, Lucas held odd jobs to keep them in food and clothing."

"I didn't know," Jennifer said softly, empathy flooding her for the young boy Lucas had once been.

"No reason why you should," Annabel said, sipping her tea, a faraway look in her eyes. "Lucas barely dated in high school, although the gossip mills were buzzing with rumors of wild parties and beautiful women after he left to travel the rodeo circuit and made a name for himself."

"Why did he stop competing in rodeos?"

"Clay died," Annabel said succinctly. "And about that same time, Wayne was diagnosed with a failing heart. In any event, Lucas came back to Butte Creek to take over running the ranch for Wayne, but when he did, he ignored women. In fact, he acts like he pretty much dislikes any female over the age of ten."

Jennifer shook her head in commiseration. "I guess you can't blame him. No wonder he acts like a grouchy bear with a sore paw most of the time. I was beginning to think it was just me who irritated him, because he clearly has excellent relationships with the men and Trey. It's a relief that it's all females and not me specifically.''

''Hmm,'' Annabel murmured noncommittally. ''Speaking of the other men,'' she said, ''what do you think of Josh? And Murphy and Charlie?''

Jennifer's smile lit her face. ''Murphy and Charlie are terrific. Murphy's smooth talk could charm the birds out of the trees, and Charlie has a smile that would melt icebergs. And Josh...'' She frowned and shrugged. ''At first I thought he disliked women in general and me in particular, but now I get the feeling that some woman hurt him and he's not coping with it at all well. I think Lucas is worried about him.''

''Really? Josh has always been a little wilder than most, but then, so was Lucas,'' Annabel said thoughtfully. ''But I do seem to remember some talk about Josh keeping company with Sarah Drummond about five months ago. And Sarah left town sometime within the last two months—just about the time that the gossip hotline started heating up with stories of Josh's fighting and drinking.''

Cindy interrupted them again, scooping up their empty plates with an easy, practiced gesture and offering dessert.

When the cheesecakes had been served, Annabel asked, ''Have you decided to stay on at Butte Creek High?''

''I'm thinking about it.'' Jennifer settled back in the booth and sipped her tea. ''It's surprising how quickly I've grown attached to the students and this town. Not to mention the beauty of the land.''

"The prairie is like the ocean—or the desert," Annabel said feelingly. "Some people see the beauty, some only see the bareness and lack of people."

"I think it's beautiful," Jennifer said, her eyes going dreamy. "There's something about being alone under all that sky. Without trees to get in the way, the land seems to roll on and on. I can't tell you the number of times I've stopped my car on top of Jones Hill just to look. I swear, I think you can see forever."

"Well, at least all the way into Canada for forty or fifty miles," Annabel said, a small smile lifting her lips. "I know what you mean, though. I used to do the same thing when I first came here and still, sometimes, it catches me unaware and takes my breath away."

The two women exchanged a smile of understanding.

An hour later, after a stop at the library, Jennifer finally made her way home, to find Beastie panting in the shade of her front porch. Hot as he was, he still greeted her with energetic exuberance.

By the time she fell into bed late Saturday evening, she was exhausted from nonstop activity and her sleepless night before. Still, tired as her body was, her mind wouldn't let her sleep.

Outside the small house, a three-quarter moon cast its light over the landscape, while inside, only the dim glow of a night-light relieved the darkness of the bedroom. Midnight had long since come and gone, and Jennifer should have been sound asleep, but the tossing and turning of her slim form beneath the bed sheets was accompanied by exasperated mutters.

"Damn!"

Jennifer sat bolt upright in bed and kicked the tangled sheets away from her legs. She squinted her eyes nearly closed and glared at the luminous dial.

"Nearly 2:00 a.m.," she groaned aloud into the silent room. She squeezed her eyes shut in frustration, then opened them wide to search the room. Her gaze found, and once again verified, the same quiet, ordinary furnishings.

"Woof?" The canine inquiry was accompanied by a cold, wet nose nudging against her palm.

Jennifer rolled her head sideways on the pillow and met the worried brown gaze of her dog.

"Sorry, Beastie," she soothed, lifting her damp palm to smooth it over the chocolate-colored Labrador's silky head. "Go back to sleep. Everything's fine."

Sighing in defeat, Jennifer straightened the crumpled bedclothes and smoothed them over the mattress. *I'm not in Seattle. I'm in Butte Creek, Montana. There's no street traffic, no police or ambulance sirens, nothing but peace and quiet. So why can't I sleep?*

She forced her muscles to lower her body flat on the bed, and she stared up at the ceiling while she counted backward from one hundred, consciously relaxing muscles from her toes upward. By the time she reached zero, she'd worked her way from toes to scalp and back down again twice. Her muscles were noticeably less tense, but sleep was still elusive. She forced her eyes closed one more time and ordered herself to fall asleep.

It didn't work.

Sighing, she gave up.

Face it, Jennifer McCleary, she thought gloomily. *It's not the lack of city noise that's keeping you awake—it's the side trip your well-ordered life has taken. It's six feet four of stubborn, impossible male. Dammit! Why did he have to kiss me? Why was I stupid enough to kiss him back?*

As a child, she had sworn not to live a life that repeated her mother's string of emotional disasters with husbands and lovers, and had focused single-mindedly on a career. She loved teaching and her inherently passionate nature found an outlet as she poured out on her students all the love and caring that she ruthlessly refused to allow in her personal life. However, her commitment to her students went beyond grading them in her classroom, and too often she'd been criticized for taking up arms in defense of a needy student.

Suddenly, the telephone rang, shattering the late-night quiet and her churning thoughts. "Who can be calling me at two in the morning?" she muttered.

She threw back the covers and scrambled out of bed, stumbling past Beastie on her way to the dark living room. The phone rang again before she could reach it and she grabbed the receiver in midring.

"Hello?"

"Jennifer? This is Lucas."

"Lucas?" She dropped into the overstuffed armchair and reached to snap on the lamp. "What is it? Is something wrong?"

"No, nothing's wrong. At least I don't think so. I'm looking for Trey. Have you seen him?"

"Trey? No, not since we finished our lessons Friday night."

"Damn."

The soft oath echoed over the line. Jennifer gripped the phone harder. "Is Trey missing? What's going on, Lucas?"

"Trey went out with some friends last night—he said he'd be back around midnight and he isn't home yet."

"But it's two in the morning—where can he be? Who were the friends?"

"Coy Beckman and Kelly Philbrick."

Jennifer's heart sank. "Oh, no. Lucas, those two are the wildest boys in school. Heaven only knows what they're up to at this hour."

"Yeah, well, I could make a guess or two."

The grim knowledge in his voice made Jennifer wince. "Maybe we should call the hospital? Or the highway patrol? They could have been in an accident."

"I've already done that," Lucas said wearily. "If they've wrecked that fancy truck of Coy's, the cops don't know about it yet."

"Oh." Jennifer tried to think. "Maybe we should go looking for them. Where were they going?"

"I don't know." Lucas's voice hardened. "I'm not that kid's daddy, and I didn't ask him. I didn't ask him what time he'd be home, either—he volunteered the information and I damn well wish he hadn't. Maybe then I wouldn't be awake at 2:00 a.m. wondering where the hell he is."

"Lucas, I'm sure there's a good reason for Trey being late."

Lucas's brief laugh was derisive. "Yeah, right, I'm sure he has a good excuse. Listen, I'm sorry I woke you. Go back to sleep. There's nothing you can do."

"Please don't be angry with him, Lucas. He's only fifteen. He probably just forgot the time."

"I'm not angry with the kid, Jennifer. If I'm mad at anybody, it's myself. I'm not Trey's father, and it's none of my business if he stays out all night—not as long as he can get up and do a full day's work tomorrow. Go back to sleep," he said again. "And forget I called. I'm sorry I woke you."

The click in her ear told her he'd hung up. Slowly, Jennifer returned the receiver to its cradle.

Going back to sleep was impossible. After an hour of tossing and turning, Jennifer gave up and rose to shower, dress and wait impatiently for the sun to rise.

At the Lazy H, Lucas didn't even attempt to go back to bed. Instead, he poured another mug of black coffee and walked out to the porch. He passed up the rocker for a straight-backed wooden chair, tilting it onto its back legs and propping his crossed ankles on the porch railing.

"What's wrong with me?" he muttered. "I should be in bed asleep, not sitting out here in the dark waiting for Clay's son to come home from God knows where."

The silence of the dark night stretched out around him while high above the earth a fat, three-quarter moon cast its pale, silver light over the rolling prairie.

Time slipped by, sliding into thirty minutes and then an hour. Lucas sipped his coffee and stared at the glittering diamond stars scattered across the black vault of sky. For what seemed like the hundredth time, he looked at his watch.

"Three o'clock. Where the hell is that kid?"

The muttered words were barely out of his mouth, when the muted growl of an engine disturbed the night's stillness.

Lucas's eyes narrowed. There was only one person in the truck that pulled up in front of the bunkhouse, and the slender figure that slid out from beneath the wheel was Trey. He didn't slam the truck door; instead, he eased it shut, the latch catching with a barely audible click. Trey took two steps toward the bunkhouse door before Lucas spoke.

"You know it's illegal to drive without a license?" His deep voice carried easily across the yard lot.

Trey froze before turning slowly to look across the intervening space.

Lucas's sharp stare assessed the teenager's reluctant steps and an unbidden surge of relief hit him when he realized that there was no stagger to Trey's walk. He waited patiently for the boy to reach the porch, and just as patiently for him to speak.

Trey halted at the foot of the steps and looked up at him. "Coy had too much to drink and was in no shape to drive," he said finally. "I figured it was better for me to drive without a license and maybe get a ticket than to let Coy drive and take the chance that he might wreck the truck."

"Hmm." Lucas's murmur of acknowledgment was noncommittal. He didn't say anything further, only sipped his coffee and watched Trey.

The teenager shifted under Lucas's unblinking stare, glancing toward the truck and silent bunkhouse and across the dark wheat fields to the county road.

"Why are you awake so late?" Trey finally burst out.

Lucas decided to tell the kid the unvarnished truth. "I was waiting till the sun came up before I called the police and started checking the ditches for wrecked trucks between here and town."

"Oh, geez." Trey's shock and guilt vibrated in his voice. He took the porch steps in two quick strides and dropped onto the edge of the rocker seat. "I didn't think you'd even know I was gone—not as long as I got home before sunup."

"I probably wouldn't have—except that you told me you'd be home by midnight and that truck of Coy's has an engine that would wake the dead. It didn't wake me."

"I always say I'll be home by midnight, but it never occurred to me that you'd wait up. My mom never knows what time I get in." Weary, bitter cynicism crept into his tone. "Even if she gets home before me, which isn't too often. And it would never occur to her to call the police or check ditches."

"Yeah, well..." Lucas stifled a biting comment about Trey's mother. "I'm not your mother. I'm not your father, either," he added, his voice going hard. "I'm your employer. And when I hired you, I made it clear that I don't put up with any alcohol use by anyone who works for me. Were you drinking with Coy?"

Trey stiffened and even in the shadows of the porch, Lucas could see the dark color that flushed his face.

"Yes, sir."

"How much?"

"I had a couple of beers with the guys. We were at a kegger at Black Bridge."

"Hmm," Lucas grunted. *Black Bridge. A couple of beers at a kegger.* He felt caught in a time warp that swapped the teenager in front of him with himself, telling Wayne Scanlon that he'd had only a few beers at a party at Black Bridge. Anger drained out of him. Wayne hadn't bothered lecturing him; instead, he'd told him not to let it happen again and then made him sling bales in a hay field for a few weeks in ninety-degree summer heat. "I ought to fire your butt off the place for breaking the rules," he said sternly.

Trey's shoulders slumped before he straightened, the effort not quite successful. "Yes, sir," he said.

"But I'm not going to."

Trey's head jerked up. "What?"

"I said, I'm not going to fire you, not if you can tell me why you drank beer when you gave me your word that you wouldn't."

Trey's blue gaze met Lucas's without flinching. "I'm not sure I can tell you why, at least not a reason that makes a lot of sense."

"Try," Lucas demanded.

"All right." Trey propped his elbows on his knees and stared down at his hands dangling between them. "Tonight was the first time I've had a beer since I started working for you—and the first time I've gone anywhere with Coy and Kelly. It's hard to explain, but the person that I am when I'm here, on the Lazy H with all of you and Miss McCleary..." He drew a deep breath and shrugged. "I'm not the same when I'm with the guys. They expect me to be like I used to be, drinking, ready to try any crazy stunt anybody thinks up." He fell silent, his shoulders tense.

Lucas waited for him to continue, but the silence lingered.

"And are you?" he prompted, his voice deep and quiet in the dark night.

"No," Trey muttered. "I'm not—but I'm not the person I am here on the Lazy H, either. To tell you the truth, I'm not sure who I am anymore. Miss McCleary tells me that I'm smart and should finish high school, go on to college. Murphy says I'd make a good cowboy. All my life, all I've ever been is the poorest kid in school, and usually the newest kid because we move around a lot. Never belonged anywhere, never thought I would. My mom, she..." He flicked a glance at Lucas, just as quickly looking away. "I guess it's no secret, she drinks sometimes."

"Yeah," Lucas said slowly, his throat constricting with a depth of emotion that threatened to stop speech. "I know. My dad drank, too, almost all the time."

"Yeah?"

"Oh, yeah." Lucas nodded, his hands clenched around the mug in his lap. "If it weren't for Wayne Scanlon, I might have ended up just like him."

"What did Wayne do?"

"He told me that every human has a choice to make—we can either repeat our parents' mistakes or we can walk our own path. We only get one shot at living—we should make damn sure it's our shot, not our parents', and not our friends'. Each man owes it to himself to think long and hard about what he wants from life."

Silence reigned on the shadowy porch. "He must have been quite a guy," Trey said finally, his voice subdued.

"Yeah," Lucas agreed. "He sure was—a hell of a man. I still miss him. I guess everyone who knew him misses him."

Trey nodded and once again, silence stretched.

"Lucas, can I ask you something?" His voice was tentative, quiet in the concealing shadows.

"You can ask—I won't guarantee I'll answer."

"What happened between you and my mom?"

Lucas tensed. "What do you mean?"

"She doesn't like you," Trey said bluntly. "But she won't tell me why."

"She won't?" Lucas let out a silent, relieved sigh. "Then I don't think I should tell you, either."

"Why not? How bad can it be? I know you went to high school with her and my dad. Didn't you like my dad?"

"Your dad was my best friend," Lucas answered swiftly, without thought.

"He was?" Trey's eyes rounded in surprise. "Then what happened? Wasn't my mom your friend, too?"

"No," he said slowly. "Your mom didn't like me very much. She thought I was a bad influence on your dad."

"Why? What did you do?"

"I followed the rodeo after high school," Lucas said reluctantly. "Clay went with me, and she wanted him to stay home."

"That's it? That's all of it? That doesn't make sense. Why would she still be mad at you after all these years?"

Lucas's mind shut down. He couldn't tell Trey that the real reason Suzie hated him was that she held him responsible for his father's death.

"I guess she thinks she has reason." Lucas lifted his boots away from the porch railing and let the chair fall back down onto all four legs. "I'm going to catch a couple of hours of sleep. You better hit the sack, too." He stood and walked to the door.

"Lucas—"

Lucas halted, the screen door half-open under his hand, and glanced over his shoulder.

"Yeah?"

"Thanks for giving me another chance. I won't let you down."

"It's more important that you don't let yourself down, son." The word came out without conscious thought.

"Yeah, well..." Trey's voice was husky and he cleared his throat before continuing. "Thanks, anyway, for the job, and for talking to me tonight. I'm sorry that you were worried—it won't happen again."

"All right. Good night." Lucas went into the house and closed the door. He heard Trey leave the porch, the sound of his boots crunching against dirt and rock growing fainter as he crossed the yard lot.

"Damn," he muttered, climbing the stairs to his bedroom. "I knew I'd be sorry for giving in to Mrs. Fitch and the teacher."

Jennifer paced the floor and waited impatiently to hear from Lucas. When the clock struck 7:00 a.m., she could wait no longer. She loaded Beastie in the passenger seat of her sports car and drove to the Lazy H.

The dog bounded out of the car and followed her, sitting alertly by her side while she knocked on the door. Jennifer couldn't wait as patiently as Beastie. She paced to the edge of the porch to take a closer look at a late-model, candy-apple red pickup truck parked outside the bunkhouse.

"I'd swear that's Coy Beckman's pickup," she muttered. "Did the boys spend the night here?"

Impatient for answers, she strode back to the door and knocked again. Her hand was in midair, ready to knock again, when the door was yanked open. Mouth open to demand answers, she gulped, swallowed and forgot what she'd been going to ask.

Lucas stood in the doorway, one hand braced on the edge of the door. His black hair was tousled, his blue eyes narrowed with sleepy irritation, and a day's growth of black beard shadowed his jaw. He was wearing a pair of faded jeans. And nothing else. It was obvious that she'd woken him from sleep. Jennifer stared in fascination at the broad expanse of his chest. Sleek brown skin smoothed over sculpted muscles; silky black hair drew a narrow line just above his navel, widening just before it disappeared beneath the worn denim that rode low on his hips.

Lucas blinked and stared at her, wondering if this was his imagination, or if she'd really stepped out of the dream he'd been having to appear on his front porch. He squinted at the angle of the morning sun over her shoulder and decided the glare was too bright to be a dream. "What are you doing here?"

His words yanked Jennifer's fascinated gaze away from hard, well-defined muscles and back to his face.

"I came to find out what happened to Trey. Did he make it home?"

"Oh, geez." Lucas scrubbed a hand over his face and gave her a lopsided, apologetic grin. "I'm sorry—I should have called you." He stood back and waved her inside. "Come on in. I need some coffee—I'm not awake yet."

Jennifer followed him down the hall and into the kitchen.

"So, tell me." Tense with concern, she dropped into a chair at the table and leaned forward, folding her arms atop the clean oak surface.

Lucas pulled open the cupboard door and took out a can of coffee. "He got home about three o'clock this morning."

"Three o'clock! Where was he till that hour?"

"At a kegger at Black Bridge."

"Oh, no." Jennifer's heart sank. She knew that Lucas had told the teenager when he hired him that drinking alcohol was forbidden. "Was he drinking?"

Lucas nodded. "Yeah."

Jennifer's eyes closed and she dropped her chin onto one hand. Her lashes lifted and she searched Lucas's impassive face. "Then I suppose you fired him." It wasn't a question; it was a weary statement of fact.

"No."

"No?" Jennifer sat bolt upright. "But I thought—Trey told me that one of the unbreakable rules for keeping this job was that he couldn't drink."

"It is—if it happens again, he's fired."

"But you gave him a second chance. Why?" Jennifer blurted out, nearly giddy with relief.

Lucas scowled at her, faint red flushing his cheeks. "Because he reminded me of myself at fifteen, that's why." A small, questioning frown creased her forehead and she looked at him expectantly. Why couldn't she leave it alone, he thought with irritation, and why did he feel the need to explain himself? He shrugged, his scowl deepening. "I was Trey's age when I did the same thing, only I had a lot more than two beers. When Wayne found out about it, he told me he'd give me one last chance, but that I had to choose between drinking and raising hell with my buddies or working for him."

"And you chose him and the Lazy H."

Her voice was soft, the look in her eyes warm with approval. Lucas shifted uncomfortably. "Don't give me too much credit. The real truth is that when I stayed out all night drinking beer, the Lazy H was in the middle of haying season and that old man had me out in the fields throwing hay bales from dawn to dusk for nearly three weeks. It damn near killed me. I didn't have time to think about partying with the boys—I didn't have the energy, either. It was all I could do to fall into bed at night and drag myself out in the morning in time to start all over again."

Jennifer chuckled, amusement bubbling in her veins to mix with heady relief. "It sounds to me as if Wayne was a pretty shrewd man."

Behind Lucas, the buzzer on the coffeemaker went off.

Jennifer stood and walked to the counter. "Are you going to send Trey out to bale hay?"

Lucas handed her a steaming mug and settled back against the counter to sip from his. His eyes closed and he sighed in sheer appreciation. "Aaah, that's good," he murmured. "What did you say?"

Jennifer sipped her own coffee and smiled at him. "I swear, you're as barely functional as I am in the morning until you have a shot of caffeine, and I thought I was the worst."

"Hmm." He lifted the cup to his mouth. "Yet another thing we have in common."

Jennifer felt heat move its way up her throat and cheeks. "Are you going to make Trey bale hay for a few weeks?"

A slow smile lifted Lucas's mouth in a devastating grin. Jennifer caught her breath and stared. His insight and concern for Trey had melted her heart; now the impact of his smile was shattering her resolve to remain uninvolved.

"It worked for me," he said, his eyes gleaming with amusement. "It might work for Trey."

"So he'll be baling hay for a while."

"No, the hay's not ready yet. But I'll think of something."

He gave her another lazy, heart-stopping grin and helplessly, Jennifer could only smile back. Beneath his gruff, tough exterior hid a man whose commitment and caring for the people he loved ran deep. Sure now that Trey had wedged a place for himself in a corner of Lucas's heart, she felt a wistful longing that there was room there for her, too.

Lucas stared at her. Her face had gone soft and warm, and the look in her eyes urged him to reach out and pull her against him. The sound of boots on the stairs stopped him.

"Mornin', Lucas." Josh walked into the kitchen and paused when he saw Jennifer. "Aren't you a little early for lessons?"

"What are you doing out of bed so early on a Sunday?" Lucas asked his brother before Jennifer could respond.

"I promised Trey we'd ride up to Shepherd's Butte today." He reached past Lucas to find a coffee mug. "I thought we'd get an early start—it's going to get hot out there."

Lucas flicked a quick glance at Jennifer, a slow grin creasing his face. "That's a great idea. Oh, and Josh?"

Josh halted at the back door and looked over at them.

"Trey's probably still asleep, but when you wake him, tell him that I think it's a good plan to go up to the butte today."

Josh scanned Lucas's grin before moving to Jennifer's twinkling eyes and amused smile. "All right," he said slowly. He left the room, shaking his head and mumbling.

"Do you think Trey will go?" Jennifer asked.

"Oh, yeah," Lucas said with absolute conviction. "He'll roll out of bed and get on that horse if it kills him—and it just might."

"No, it won't kill him," Jennifer disagreed. "He'll just wish he was dead before noon."

Lucas's deep chuckle joined her peal of laughter. She set her coffee cup on the counter and was drying her eyes, before she realized he'd gone silent. When she looked up, his intent blue stare spoke volumes.

Chapter Seven

Jennifer wanted nothing more than to step into Lucas's arms. But the strength of the pull toward him was a sharp warning of the danger that lay there.

"I guess I should be going," she managed to say.

"Yeah," Lucas answered. The early-morning sun slanted through the windows, finding gold strands in the loose mane of her red-gold hair. His fingertips tingled, remembering the feel of the silky mass. A night with too little sleep had smudged faint, dark circles of weariness in the fragile skin beneath her eyes, and beneath the toasty gold of summer tan, her fair skin was paler than usual. He felt a flash of guilt that his telephone call had wakened her and no doubt caused her sleeplessness. "Why don't you have breakfast first?" he offered. She started to shake her head in refusal, but he ignored her. "It's the least I can do after waking you in the middle of the night and worrying you."

"It's not your fault I couldn't sleep," Jennifer assured him. "I've never been able to master the art of turning off worry even when I know very well that there's nothing I can do."

Lucas wasn't convinced, but decided to let it go. "Stay and have breakfast, anyway."

Jennifer tilted her head and stared at him speculatively, a small smile growing. "Is this a friendly gesture or do you want me to cook breakfast?"

"Hell, no," he growled. "I can cook my own breakfast—and yours. I'm not completely useless in the kitchen."

"Then this is a friendly gesture?"

"Yeah," he muttered, shooting her a frown that turned into a slow grin. "We called a truce and decided to be friends, right?" Her nod of agreement had him pushing away from the cabinet. "So, friend, you can stay and have breakfast with me. Then you can feed carrots to Maggie while I fix the fence and replace a post in the home pasture."

"All right," Jennifer said, giving in with a dazzling smile. Sharing their worry over Trey had broken down barriers between them and Lucas seemed less remote, more approachable. He was treating her with the same relaxed, easy friendliness that she'd seen between him and Murphy, and the prospect of spending the morning with this warmer version of the rancher was too enticing to refuse.

"Great." He ran a hand over the rough black stubble shadowing his jaw and glanced down at himself. "I'll shave and get dressed." He shot her a threatening glare. "And I'm making breakfast, so don't move until I get back."

Jennifer laughed. "Yes, sir. Is it all right if I sit on the porch and finish my coffee while I'm waiting?" she called after him.

"Yeah." His deep voice carried back to her as he disappeared down the hall to the stairs.

Jennifer stepped out onto the wide front porch. Dropping into the rocking chair, she rested her head against the high wooden back and, with her eyes half-closed against the morning sun, she sipped her coffee and gazed out across quiet, rolling acres of the Lazy H.

The sun was more hot than warm on her toes in their leather sandals and its rays heated her forearms, bare beneath the rolled-up sleeves of her white cotton shirt. She was half-asleep, her thoughts drifting lazily in the warm morning air, when she heard the clatter of boots on the stairway inside.

"Hey, you." Lucas's deep voice came through the screen door. "Are you asleep?"

Jennifer smiled, long strands of her hair shifting over her shoulder when she turned her head sideways to look at him. "No, but if you'd been another five minutes, I would have been."

Lucas felt his muscles tighten. Sunlight poured over her slim form curled into the big old rocker. Tiny freckles were scattered across the bridge of her nose, her bare arms tanned a pale gold by the summer sun. Her hair was more gold than red under the sun's rays and reminded him, not for the first time, that she was a woman of sunshine and warmth. The urge to bask in that warmth and capture some of that sunshine for himself was strong.

"I guess it's lucky I didn't take another five minutes," he said as he pushed open the door. "Are you going to sleep out here in the sun or come inside and help me make breakfast?"

She didn't move. He'd shaved, and his hair, still damp from the shower, gleamed a soft, dull black. Handsome as he was in the pale blue shirt tucked into the waistband of clean jeans with black cowboy boots covering his feet, a part of her wished that he was still bare-chested. But she didn't tell him. Instead, she smiled lazily at him. "I thought you said you were cooking breakfast?"

"I did. I am. But I never said that you couldn't help."

Jennifer stretched with indolent grace. "All right, but you have to fry the bacon. I hate dealing with spattering bacon grease."

"Deal."

Lucas held the door and followed her down the hall to the kitchen.

An hour later, he loaded the last of the dirty dishes into the dishwasher and crossed to the refrigerator.

"Do you want to try feeding Maggie her carrots again?" he asked, glancing over the top of the open door at her. She wrinkled her nose and looked doubtful. "She's not going to bite you as long as you remember to keep your hand flat."

"Actually, what I'd really like to do is fall asleep in the sun."

"We'll say hello to Maggie first, then you can take a nap—but not in the sun, it's too hot. You can use a bed in the house or the hay in the barn, if you want."

Jennifer thought about sleeping in his bed, even alone, and immediately rejected the idea. She wasn't convinced she wanted to chance feeding Maggie, either, but she nodded reluctantly. "All right, but if I lose a finger along with a carrot, I'm blaming you."

"If she takes a finger with a carrot, you'll be in too much pain to blame me," he said dryly. He grabbed a handful of carrots and closed the door. "Come on, let's go see the baby."

It was after 10:00 a.m. when they left the house and strolled across the yard lot, and the sun had picked up heat, beating down on their heads.

"Josh was right," Jennifer commented, squinting up at the sun in the bright blue, cloudless sky. "It's going to be a scorcher today."

"Yup," Lucas agreed, tilting his own head back. The shade of his Stetson brim protected his eyes, but the hot sun's glare still had his eyes squinting. He glanced at Jennifer and frowned. "You need a hat," he said. "Hasn't anybody warned you not to run around in Montana summer heat without a hat? This isn't Seattle. Next thing I know, Doc Hansen will be treating you for sunstroke." He lifted the black cowboy hat from his head and dropped it on Jennifer's.

Startled, she looked up at him. He was frowning at her, but for the first time, she realized that his irritation was because he cared. She felt cherished and protected; both feelings were so rare in her experience with men that it took her several moments to realize what they were.

"Thanks."

"No problem." Lucas was stunned by the swift, blinding force of her smile. "It's a little big," he drawled. "We'll have to get you one that fits."

"All right," she agreed. She glanced down at her feet, where her pink-tipped toes were bare in strappy flat sandals. "And I think it's time I bought some boots, too."

Lucas grinned at the feminine toes and the impractical strips of narrow leather. "That's not a bad idea, especially if you're going to visit Maggie and her baby on a regular basis."

Jennifer glanced at the thin soles on her sandals and grimaced. "I see what you mean—I certainly couldn't shovel manure in these, could I?"

"Are you interested in shoveling manure?" he retorted with quick interest. "I could always use a volunteer in the barn."

"Nice try, but I don't think so, Lucas," she said dryly. "I didn't say I *wanted* to clean stalls."

He chuckled, and once again, Jennifer was struck with how handsome he was when he smiled, the stern lines of his face softening, his blue eyes crinkling at the corners. Relaxed, Lucas Hightower was a potent threat to any female, and Jennifer knew she was far from immune.

She forced her attention over the wheat fields to the rise of Shepherd's Butte in the distance. Beyond the alternating strips of ripening wheat and bare, plowed, fallow land stretched the rougher pasture grass that surrounded the base of the butte. As she watched, two riders on horseback paused to open and shut a gate before angling away from the fence line.

"Lucas," she asked, pointing toward the butte, "is that Josh and Trey?"

"Yeah, must be." He lifted a hand to shade his eyes. "And if I'm not mistaken, that's your dog with them."

"You're kidding!" Jennifer watched the distant riders until she caught the movements of a third, smaller animal that was clearly a dog—a big, dark-colored dog. "Oh, for heaven's sake. It never occurred to me that Beastie might follow them. Will he be all right?"

Lucas glanced down at her exasperated, worried face. "Sure, he'll be fine. Josh and Trey will look out for him, although he'll be one tired dog by the time they get home."

"When do you think they'll be back?"

"Not for several hours. Josh is going to check on the cattle and the spring in the hills south of the butte."

"Why do you call it Shepherd's Butte? You don't have sheep up there, do you?"

"Not now." Lucas's sweeping gesture indicated the miles of prairie surrounding them. "But when all of this land was open range, long before this part of Montana was homesteaded, sheepmen would leave Great Falls in the summer with a couple of thousand sheep in a band and graze them on free grass across the northern part of Montana before they sold them, fat and healthy, when they reached North Dakota. Along the way, the shepherds would climb the highest buttes and leave a stone, sometimes with their name and the date scratched on the rock. Over the years, the stacks of stones got higher and higher."

Fascinated, Jennifer squinted at the distant butte, trying in vain to find a pillar of stones on its high top. "Is there still a mound of stones up there?"

Lucas nodded. "Yup. Nearly as high as my waist. You can read the dates on some of the sandstone rocks from as far back as the late 1800s."

"I'd love to see them. Can I ride up there someday?"

"Can you ride?"

"Yes. Not as well as you, I'm sure, but I think I could manage."

"How did you learn to ride if you've lived in a city as big as Seattle all your life?"

"One of my mother's husbands liked horses, and he taught me."

"*One* of her husbands?" Lucas's glance was surprised and curious. "How many did she have?"

"Three." Jennifer's vivid expression shuttered and she turned away from her contemplation of the butte. "Why do you call Maggie's colt 'Baby'? Haven't you picked out a name for him yet?"

"Nope, not yet." Lucas let her get away with the abrupt change of subject, but made a mental note to find out why she froze when the subject of her mother's husbands came up. He reached out and caught her arm when she would have turned toward the open doors to the barn. "Maggie and her baby are out in the pasture. Wait here a minute, I'll be right back."

A moment later, he returned. "Here, try this."

Jennifer turned just as he plucked the black Stetson off her head. Before she could protest, he plopped a smaller, straw cowboy hat in its place and tugged the brim down over her forehead.

"Looks like the size is about right. How does it feel?"

Jennifer tugged experimentally on the brim and shifted it back a little. "Great—whose is it?"

"Murphy's. His niece left it in his truck when she was visiting."

"Do you think she'll mind if I wear it?"

Lucas shot her an amused half grin. "No," he drawled. "It's been in the tack room for the last three years, I don't think she's likely to show up in the next few minutes and claim it."

"Oh."

He settled his own black Stetson over his forehead and held out his hand. "Here, carry this for me, will you?"

Jennifer accepted the wooden carpenter's carrier, surprised by its weight. It held tools, including a hammer, and an assortment of nails and staples. "What are you going to do with this?"

Lucas easily shouldered a posthole digger and two metal fence posts. "I have to replace two of the fence posts in the pasture. You can feed Maggie her treat while I fix the fence."

"Hmph." Jennifer gave him a wry look. "I should have known you wouldn't actually go a whole two hours without working. Do you ever take a whole day off?"

"Sure." He steered her toward the far end of the corral and the pasture where Maggie was grazing, her little colt close at hand. "In August of every year, I go to the county fair."

Jennifer set the carrier on the ground and gingerly closed her fingers over the fence's top strand of barbed wire to watch Baby as he investigated a clump of grama grass. He snorted at the grass and raced off across the pasture before rocketing back to his mother's side, his short tail flying in the wind created by his passing, his long legs seemingly too long for his compact body.

"He's something, isn't he?"

Lucas's amused comment held an unmistakable note of pride. Jennifer glanced at him. The hot sun poured over him, finding iridescent streaks in his black hair and gleaming off the bronze tan of his skin.

She looked over at the colt and chuckled. "His coat is the same color as your hair."

"Oh, yeah?" A slow grin tilted his mouth and he leaned one forearm on a fence post, the other hand propped negligently on his hip as he stared at the mare and her baby. "I'm not sure if I should be flattered or insulted, considering that you're comparing me to a horse."

"What will you do with him?" Jennifer asked curiously. "Will you keep him or sell him?"

"I'll keep him," Lucas answered instantly. "Josh has been after me to try breeding quarter horses and Baby has all the right bloodlines for a stud."

"Is Josh good with horses?"

"The best." A brief frown curved Lucas's hard mouth downward and he looked off toward the butte where Josh and Trey were small moving figures, just barely visible. "Six months ago breeding quarter horses was about all Josh could talk about."

"Six months ago?" Jennifer asked, wondering at the worry lines bracketing Lucas's mouth. "What happened?"

"A woman happened." Lucas flicked her a hard, unreadable glance. "At least I think it's a woman that's driving him crazy."

"A woman?" Jennifer recalled her conversation with Annabel. "Someone mentioned that Josh used to date Sarah Drummond—is that the woman you mean?"

"What town gossip told you about Sarah?" Lucas asked, his relaxed stance disappearing as he straightened away from the fence, his jaw hard, his gaze forbidding.

"I don't remember." Jennifer told the white lie without a twinge of conscience.

"What else did this person whose name you can't remember tell you?"

"Only that Josh was keeping company with Sarah and that she left town about the same time that he started getting into fights and drinking more than usual."

"Drinking more than usual?" Lucas's body tightened, his blue eyes turning wintry. "Are you sure they didn't tell you that he's following in his father's footsteps?"

"No," Jennifer denied swiftly, "they didn't."

"Then maybe they told you that everyone always knew that those Hightower boys would turn out bad, it was only a matter of time? Or that blood always tells, and God knows, Josh has more than enough bad blood, not to mention bad genes?" he said derisively.

"Aren't you jumping to conclusions? Just because someone mentioned Josh and Sarah doesn't necessarily mean that they said anything derogatory," Jennifer retorted.

"Sure it does," he drawled flatly. "In this county, Josh and I will always be Will Hightower's sons, and that means every mother's son expects us to turn into the town drunks. Just like our father."

"That's ridiculous," Jennifer said crisply. Anger boiled beneath the ice of his stare, but she met it without flinching. "No one believes that about either you or Josh. If they did, why would Annabel have asked you to hire Trey this summer? She would never have sent a vulnerable, troubled boy to a man she didn't trust."

Lucas waved a dismissing hand. "Annabel isn't like the rest of the world—she never has been. I can guarantee you that Patricia Drummond didn't approve of Josh dating her daughter."

"That still doesn't mean that everyone in Butte Creek thinks badly of you and Josh," Jennifer said.

Lucas shook his head in disgust. "Teacher, you just don't get it, do you? This is a small town and people never forget. They don't forget who your parents were or what kind of trouble you stirred up when you were a teenager, and it doesn't make any difference that you might have changed. No matter how hard you try and how long you live, you can't make them change their minds."

"And so you just gave up? Even knowing that you're not responsible for what your father may have done or how he chose to live his life?" Jennifer was furious with him.

"No, I didn't give up. I just stopped caring what anyone thought." Lucas picked up the fence posts and posthole digger. "I have to fix the fence. Feel free to use any bed in the house or the hay in the barn loft to take a nap. I'll let you know when Josh and Trey get back with your dog."

Jennifer watched in frustration as he turned his back on her and stalked off down the fence line. He was nearly a hundred yards away, when he stopped, dropped the posts and posthole digger to the ground, and went to work.

She frowned and turned her back on him to march to the barn. The interior was dim and cool, much cooler than the steadily climbing temperature outside. Halfway down the aisle to the box stalls where she'd first seen Maggie and the colt, a ladder was built against the wall, its rungs disappearing above her through a square opening in the ceiling. She grasped a rung and set one sandaled foot on the lowest rung, moving cautiously up the ladder until she could step into the loft. The back half of the open expanse held stacked bales, but at the front of the barn, near a big open door, the loose hay from broken bales had been tossed.

Jennifer walked across the hay-strewn rough planks and stood in the four-foot-wide doorway. From this height, she had a view of the ranch buildings and a distractingly clear view of Lucas. He was shirtless in the heat and the sun gleamed off his shoulders. The muscles across his back flexed and bunched as he drove the posthole digger into the ground, the pile of dirt beside the hole growing steadily bigger as she watched.

He is the stubbornnest, most impossible man I have ever known!

A yawn caught her by surprise and she blinked, abruptly overcome with weariness. She tugged the straw hat off her head and glanced around the huge loft until she found several horse blankets stacked atop a hay bale.

"It's a good thing I'm not allergic to dust," she said aloud as she shook out one of the blankets, then spread it over a mound of hay near the door. Stretched out on the blanket near the open barn door, she could see Lucas laboring over the fence, the buttes in the distance and the hot blue sky beyond and above it all. A faint breeze drifted through the door, carrying the scents of sage and ripening wheat. Contentment filled her and she drifted off to sleep.

Lucas knew she was in the barn. He'd glanced over his shoulder when she left Maggie and the colt at the fence and seen her cross the threshold. When she didn't come back, he figured she must have chosen the loft and the soft hay as a place to take a nap instead of a bed in the house. By the time he'd finished replacing the fence posts, a nap didn't sound like a bad idea. He doubted that he'd gotten even three hours of sleep the night before.

Besides, he owed Jennifer an apology for snarling at her when she'd asked him about Josh. At least that's what he told himself when he put the tools away in the barn and climbed the ladder to the loft.

Whatever reasoning he'd used to seek her out fled his mind entirely when he stepped into the loft and saw her.

She was sound asleep, curled on her side away from him and facing the open loft door. Her hair was a fan of red-gold silk against the blue canvas she lay on and her fair skin was flushed and dewy with perspiration from the heat.

Lucas crossed the wood-plank floor and leaned against the doorjamb to look down at her. The loft was shaded from the midday sun, but dust motes danced in the golden shafts of sunlight that found their way through the cracks in the rough board siding. She stirred as he watched, the thick fans of her eyelashes fluttering before she settled into sleep once again, one jean-covered knee shifting higher against the canvas. He followed the movement, his gaze continuing up her thigh to trace the stretch of soft, worn denim from her knee to the outward curve of her bottom and the inward curve of her waist. White lace and lightly tanned, soft skin was just visible in the vee of the tailored white cotton shirt she wore.

Lucas had never been more tempted. But the pale shadows smudged beneath her eyes cooled the heat in his veins.

Aw, hell, he conceded wearily. She was tired—he was tired—and he didn't have the heart to wake her. The apology, and anything else, could wait until she was awake and they were both rested.

He lowered himself quietly onto the canvas next to her, stretched his long legs out beside hers, tipped his hat forward over his eyes and went to sleep.

Jennifer was dreaming. Like all of her dreams since meeting Lucas, this dream was about the big rancher. Except in this dream, she was lying in his arms on a soft bed that rustled beneath them. A smile curved her mouth and she stretched, snuggling closer.

"You do that again and I won't be responsible for the consequences."

The deep, husky murmur stirred the hair just above her ear and Jennifer's eyes flew open.

"You're not a dream," she whispered inanely against the warm skin of Lucas's throat. Her cheek lay against the blue cotton of his shirt, her face snuggled into the curve where throat met shoulder. Her fingers flexed experimentally, testing the resiliency of solid chest muscles.

The hard arms encircling her tightened instinctively in response, pressing her closer to the warm body she lay against. Her fingers stilled and she blinked slowly, her brain still fuzzed with sleep, while she struggled to grasp her surroundings and realized that she was draped across Lucas's prone body. Her head was tucked against his shoulder, her breasts pressed against his chest, her jeans zipper aligned with his hipbone. One leg was bent and draped over the powerful muscles of his thigh, her knee nudging him just below his belt buckle.

"How did you get here?" she asked, her voice a hushed murmur. "You weren't here when I went to sleep."

"I finished fixing the fence and came looking for you," Lucas answered, his own voice raspy. "You were already sound asleep and you looked so comfortable, I decided to catch up on lost sleep myself."

Jennifer considered his words for a moment. "Why am I lying nearly on top of you?"

Lucas went completely still. "I'm not sure," he said carefully. "I woke up and there you were."

"Oh." Jennifer wondered briefly why she had turned trustingly to him in her sleep. She moved experimentally against him, pressing closer, and he instantly responded with that same tightening of muscles. His hands, one against her back, the other cupping the curve of her hip, moved in slow, testing circles, pressing her gently against him in rhythmic surges. His breath was coming more quickly, his chest rising and falling beneath her hand. With other men, faster breathing had only meant a warning for her to quickly say good-night. With Lucas, she didn't want to leave, and the need to explore her own speeding pulse was too strong to refuse. "Lucas," she said slowly. "Do I need to apologize?"

"Apologize? For what?"

"For this." She shifted against him, lifting her head to look up at him, and he groaned softly, his fingers clenching gently. "We decided that we were going to be just friends, and I'm not sure that climbing on top of you when you're asleep is allowed between friends."

"Honey, you can climb on top of me anytime you want to," he said huskily.

His eyes were half-closed, their expression nearly hidden behind black lashes, but Jennifer could read the arousal in his eyes as easily as she could feel the heat that poured from him.

"What is it about you?" she murmured aloud, perplexed, her usual reserve swamped by the enormity of what she was feeling. Baffled by the odd combination of safety and excitement she felt in his arms, she frowned at him. "I've never felt this way with anyone else." Her frown deepened accusingly. "And I'm not sure I like it."

Lucas ignored the last half of her declaration and focused on the first half. "You've never felt what way?"

Jennifer stared at him for a long moment while she struggled to put into words what she barely understood herself. "Bothered," she said finally.

Lucas's hands stilled. "Bothered? What does that mean?"

"It means my body goes haywire around you—I have trouble breathing, my stomach gets a pack of butterflies flying around inside. You know, bothered. But on the other hand, I feel safe, as if lying on top of you is a perfectly normal, natural place for me to be." She shifted against him and her knee nudged his jeans zipper. She didn't have any trouble understanding exactly what was happening to him beneath that zipper and she lifted an eyebrow at him. "And *safe* is the last thing I should be feeling."

"You're just as safe as you want to be," he said softly. "I've never forced a woman in my life—we'll never do anything you don't want to do."

"That's part of the problem," she said, her own voice hushed and throaty. "I find myself wanting to do all sorts of things with you that I've never wanted to do with anyone else. And that's not wise, because we both know we're absolutely wrong for each other."

"You're right," Lucas agreed solemnly. "We are." He stared at her flushed face for a long moment. "What kind of things?" The reluctant, softly growled question was pulled from him by overwhelming curiosity.

She didn't answer, but the color staining her cheeks darkened, and her gaze dropped to his mouth. Lucas felt the imperceptible easing of her body closer against his and groaned.

"Is kissing one of the things you want? There isn't any law that says friends can't kiss each other," he said gently, reading the leap of heated response and wary indecision in her eyes. "We both know that this isn't going anywhere, so what's the harm?"

The temptation to give in was strong. Not only was every nerve in her body urging her to accept his offer, but strangely, his agreement that there was no possibility that either of them would allow the incredible heat between them to develop further than a few kisses was reassuring.

"Show me," he said, his deep voice raspy and barely audible. "Show me what kind of things you want."

Jennifer was barely aware of the drag of her body against his as his powerful hands tugged her upward the few inches necessary to poise her face above his. She cast aside caution and recklessly lowered her head.

His lips were warm and amazingly soft, the taste of his mouth erotic beneath hers, and Jennifer's eyes drifted closed.

The soft, lush heat of her mouth on his was driving Lucas crazy. She didn't seem to notice when he shifted her body atop his and wrapped her tighter. She only murmured with satisfaction and pressed closer, giving a little wiggle of adjustment that nestled the cove of her hips against his.

Lucas broke out in a fine sweat, closed his fist over a handful of thick, silky hair and struggled to remember that this was her fantasy.

It didn't work. Her fantasy was too much like his. When she lifted her mouth from his and gasped, drawing air into breathless lungs, his chest was heaving with his own effort to breathe. He opened his eyes and looked up at her, but caught only a glimpse of faintly swollen lips and dazed, sultry eyes before she began brushing butterfly kisses over his face, closing his eyelids with the soft stroke of her lips.

He withstood the subtle torture for as long as he could, but when her mouth explored his ear and moved down his jaw to his throat to find and linger on the pulse that beat there, Lucas could bear no more.

"My turn," he muttered, and rolled with her until she was beneath him, staring up at him with eyes heavy-lidded with desire. Holding her gaze, he slowly bent and brushed a kiss against the damp curve of her lips. "Open your mouth, baby." His voice was raspy, guttural with need. "Let me in."

The tip of his tongue stroked against the seam of her lips and Jennifer shuddered. There was no denying the sexually explicit, half demand, half plea of male to female in his voice, in the fit of his hard body over hers.

She gave in, relishing the violent shudder that shook his body when she opened her mouth, welcoming the invasion with an eagerness that would have shocked her were she capable of realizing the depth of her response.

"Lucas! Hey, Lucas, are you in here?"

Lucas froze, his hands and arms tightening around Jennifer, before he lifted his head, just enough to take his mouth from hers.

"Did you find Lucas, Josh?" Trey's tenor floated up through the open barn door and into the loft.

Chapter Eight

"He doesn't answer," Josh told Trey, his voice fading as he walked through the barn and growing stronger as he exited and stopped outside beneath the open window. "His truck's here, so maybe he's up at the house. Why don't you unsaddle the horses and rub them down while I go see if I can find him."

"Sure."

Bits jingled, the creak of leather clearly audible over the murmur of Trey's voice as he talked to the horses.

"Damn," Lucas whispered with heartfelt frustration.

He dropped his forehead to the canvas next to Jennifer's temple, his cheek against hers, his labored breathing rasping in her ear. Jennifer realized that her arms were around his neck and her fingers threaded tightly in the silky thickness of his hair.

"They're back," she said with a sigh, forcing her fingers to release their hold. Her hands slid caressingly from his hair to link together loosely at his nape.

He lifted his head and looked down at her. The clear disappointment on her expressive features told him he wasn't alone in his frustration.

"Yeah," he said. "We'll wait until Trey goes up to the house before we leave." He gently brushed a wispy red-gold curl from her cheek and lingered to stroke her soft skin. "My brother always has had lousy timing."

She arched an eyebrow at him. "Does this happen to you often? Being caught in the hay loft with a woman?"

"Hell, no," he denied swiftly. Her eyes held more than a hint of vulnerability and his hand stilled on her cheek. "It's been a long, long time since I've been with a woman, in a hayloft or anywhere else."

Jennifer's heart leaped at his words, the straightforward declaration soothing her uncertainty. "I'm glad I'm not the only one who doesn't make a practice of rolling around in the hay with strange men," she said quietly.

He grinned at her choice of phrasing. "Well, now, honey, I doubt I'd ever be interested in a roll in the hay with a strange man," he drawled. "On the other hand," he said, brushing his thumb over her bottom lip, "anytime you get the notion, I'd be glad to oblige."

"You have no idea just how often I get the notion," she said dryly, trying to ignore the frissons of heated excitement that shivered through her at his touch. Her fingers moved in unconscious caresses against his nape and drew an answering shudder from him.

"So tell me," he said huskily, his eyes narrowing over her face.

"I don't think so."

"Then I'll just have to assume that you think about kissing me as often as I think about kissing you, which is every time I see you."

Startled, her eyes widened and she stared at him. The unmistakable signs of arousal were easily readable in the hot blue of heavy-lidded eyes and the flush that stained the hard thrust of his cheekbones. His lips were faintly swollen from the kisses they'd shared, his thick black hair ruffled by her restless fingers.

"We're in trouble," she breathed, hardly realizing that she'd said the words aloud.

"Why?"

"Because this isn't safe, for either of us," she said quickly. "If you're going through the same hormonal surges that I am, which one of us is going to keep us from crossing the line?"

"What line?"

"The line between hot kisses and making love."

Lucas figured that at the rate they were going, that line was going to blur past recognition in no time. "If you're worried about this getting out of hand before we can stop, then maybe we should use the old high-school rule."

"What high-school rule?"

"The one about legal above the waist, illegal below." He lifted a curious eyebrow at her shocked look. "Honey, did you date at all in high school? Or were the boys you knew all slow?"

"Of course I dated." She frowned at him. "I didn't date the school studs, but that doesn't mean that there was anything wrong with the boys I went out with. They were all very nice.''

Lucas groaned. ''Nice? That word is the kiss of death.'' A sudden, startling thought occurred to him and his gaze sharpened. ''You have done this before, haven't you?''

''Done what?'' she asked warily.

''You know what,'' he said impatiently. ''Had sex. Made love. Had—what did you call it? Oh, yeah, hormonal surges.''

Jennifer didn't want to tell him. But given the fact that they'd gone from being adversaries to sharing a strange form of friendship, then swiftly advanced to hot kisses and screaming hormones, she reluctantly decided she might as well.

''Yes, I've had sex,'' she said precisely. ''No, I've never made love, and no, I've never suffered from hormonal surges before.''

Lucas stared at her silently for a moment, trying to sort out her response. ''How did you manage to have sex without hormonal urges?''

Embarrassed color heated her cheeks. ''I met a nice guy when I was in my junior year in college. We dated and talked about getting married. We had so much in common, and I really cared for him, but when I finally gave in and we had sex, it was just . . .''

''Nothing?'' he offered when she hesitated. ''No fireworks? No skyrockets?''

''No skyrockets, no fireworks,'' she agreed. ''He didn't even argue when I didn't want to repeat it.''

''But college was a few years ago, right?'' Lucas waited for her nod of agreement. ''You must have met some guy since then who set off fireworks.''

"No." Jennifer shook her head slowly, her hair shifting against the blue canvas. "I've dated nice guys but... Actually, until I met you, I thought I had my hormones well trained and behaving themselves."

"There hasn't been anyone since, has there?" She shook her head, and his eyes narrowed as the implication of her answer hit him. "Damn," he breathed. "You're a virgin."

"I am not," she denied quickly.

"Technically, no," he agreed. "But in all the ways that count, you are. Damn." He squeezed his eyes closed and dropped his head to the canvas, burying his face in the silky fan of her hair.

Jennifer lay perfectly still, staring up at the open beams of the roof. Her traitorous body was reacting to the press of his, heating and stirring, her nipples pebbling against the lace of her bra where his chest crowded hers.

"I fail to see why my having had sex on only one, eminently forgettable, occasion should be so upsetting to you," she said with irritation.

"That's because you're a virgin."

The muttered reply was muffled by her hair. Jennifer shifted her head sideways to look at him, her nose only inches from his cheek. "What does that have to do with understanding you?" she demanded.

Lucas turned his head until they were nose-to-nose. "Because if you knew more about men and sex, you'd know that telling a man that he makes you hot and that you're a virgin is like waving a red flag in front of a bull. Especially when you've just kissed him until he's nearly crazy."

"Oh."

They stared silently at each other.

"I should have known that," she said with conviction.

"Yeah, you should have," he agreed.

"This only reinforces my original statement," she said. "These—displays of affection aren't safe for our emotional equilibrium."

Lucas lifted his head and braced his weight on his forearms to look down at her. "Teacher, you have the damnedest way of saying things. I assume what you call 'displays of affection' is a polite way to refer to the fact that we've just kissed each other till we're both ready to go off like rockets?"

"If you want to be blunt—yes," she said tightly. "I was trying to be polite."

"Whatever," he growled dismissingly. "I've already told you that you're just as safe with me as you want to be."

"I don't know," she began doubtfully.

"I do," he said shortly. "You've got me hotter than a two-dollar pistol, lady. If there were any possibility that I'd ever rip off your clothes and jump your bones without your wanting me to, you'd be naked under me right now and I'd be buried so deep inside you that you'd think we were fused for life."

"Oh." Jennifer breathed, mesmerized by the burning conviction in his blue eyes. The hard ridge of his body where he lay wedged between her thighs underlined his words with heart-stopping clarity. "Well, then, umm, I guess we're safe as long as we follow the rule of . . . what was that rule again?"

"Legal above the waist, illegal below the waist?"

"Yes, I think that's what you said."

Lucas's eyes flared with heat. His gaze left hers and flicked to the vee of smooth skin and the wisp of lace visible above the top button of her blouse. His fingers curled as if they already cupped the rise of her breast beneath the white cotton.

"Not now," he muttered to himself. A man could only take so much and his body was already screaming for completion. It was the wrong place and the wrong time, for he'd heard Trey turn the horses into the corral several moments before. He didn't dare touch her again; if he did, he doubted he'd know if Josh returned and set off a cannon next to them.

"What was that?" Jennifer asked.

"Hmm?" Lucas lifted his gaze to hers.

"What did you say?"

"Nothing—Trey's gone, it's safe to go down now."

He moved off her and rolled to his feet, reaching down to catch her hands in his and pull her up to stand in front of him.

"You've got hay in your hair," he said gruffly. He carefully tugged a short alfalfa stem from her hair and brushed the silky strands back over her shoulder before he turned abruptly and swept his Stetson and her borrowed straw hat from the floor. He settled his own black hat on his head and handed her the smaller straw one.

"I'll go down the ladder first," he told her, frowning at the slick-soled sandals she was wearing. "If you slip, I can catch you."

"All right." She settled the straw hat on her head and followed him to the ladder, waiting until he'd stepped down several rungs before she followed him.

His legs were longer than hers and even though she was two rungs above him on the ladder, still his waist was even with hers, his arms circling her, his hands just below hers on the ladder. Her back brushed against the broad, solid bulk of his chest and she felt cherished, protected and safe.

In all her twenty-eight years, she had sought out, coveted and cherished her hard-won independence. This odd urge to rest on another's strength was disconcerting.

"Woof."

The deep, inquisitive bark halted them three rungs from the bottom of the ladder and they both looked over their shoulders at the barn floor below. Beastie lay stretched out, panting, as he watched them expectantly.

Lucas looked from the dog to Jennifer. She was staring at the Lab with consternation and her gaze slowly swung to his.

"Do you think he's been there all this time?" she asked softly.

"I don't think so," Lucas responded. "I heard him bark when Josh went to the house—he probably went with him."

"I hope so. If he's been lying there since Josh and Trey came back, they must have known that we were up in the loft."

"Don't worry about it," Lucas assured her, moving down the last of the rungs to the floor. He reached up and caught her by the waist, swinging her down beside him. "Josh wouldn't have missed the opportunity to tease us if he'd known we were up there."

One hand resting on her waist, he held her in front of him and smoothed her hair back over her shoulder. "If he says anything to you, tell me and I'll take care of it."

"Josh wouldn't purposely say anything to embarrass me, Lucas," she reassured him.

"He wouldn't normally, but he pretty much hates women in general lately and he might hurt you without meaning to. If he does, tell me."

"All right." Jennifer traced the line of one black eyebrow with her finger and cupped her palm over his cheek. Lucas's eyes drifted nearly closed and he covered her hand with his, holding it tightly against his skin before he turned his face and pressed a kiss into her palm.

"No more, honey." His voice was raw with need when he drew her hand away from his lips. "If I'm going to make it through the day, you'd better go home."

Jennifer walked beside him out of the barn and into the hot sunlight, Beastie at her heels.

"Hey, Lucas!"

They were halfway across the yard lot when Josh exited the house and saw them.

Lucas waved in response and Josh and Trey met them at Jennifer's car.

"Where have you two been?" Josh asked.

"In the pasture behind the barn, checking the water in the horse trough. Is everything okay up at the butte?" Lucas held open the car door and waited till Jennifer and Beastie were settled inside before closing it firmly behind them. His face held nothing but mild inquiry when he turned to look at Josh.

"Yeah, everything's fine." Josh's gaze flicked from Jennifer to Lucas. "Trey and I chased a bull and two steers of Hildebrand's back through a hole in the fence on the south side. We came to get wire and new posts to fix it."

Lucas cursed softly. "When the hell is he going to get rid of that damn bull? Every time we turn around, he finds a way through that fence! I'm tired of replacing it. If that old codger spent half as much time watching his livestock as he spends watching us, that damn bull wouldn't give us nearly as much grief.''

''True.'' Josh shoved his hat back on his head and looked at the sky. ''We'd better go and get new barbed wire up before he's back on our side of the fence again.''

''I'll come with you,'' Lucas said. ''Between the three of us, we should be able to replace it before Murphy and Charlie get home.''

''Right.'' Josh bent at the waist and peered in the car window. ''Nice to see you, Jennifer.''

''Nice to see you, too, Josh,'' she replied calmly. She met his suspicious gaze with an open, straightforward stare and knew a flash of relief when he nodded abruptly and turned away.

''See you tomorrow night,'' Trey said and smiled, waiting for Jennifer's nod of agreement before he turned and hurried off after Josh.

Lucas bent over to look in the window at her. ''Drive carefully.''

''I will.''

''Maybe tomorrow night, after Trey's lesson, you can stay a while?''

''I'd like that.'' Jennifer's smile was tremulous.

''Great.'' His gaze held hers for a moment longer, before he stuck his hands into the back pockets of his jeans, straightened and stepped back from the car. ''See you tomorrow.''

''Bye.'' Jennifer turned the ignition key and shifted the little car into gear. The rearview mirror told her that he stood, watching her drive away, until she turned onto the county road and could no longer see him.

Jennifer worried that Lucas might have second thoughts. By Monday evening, her nerves were strung tight, but the men trooped into the house, starved, as usual, and loudly appreciative of dinner, and Lucas was neither more nor less friendly than any other night.

When he disappeared immediately after dinner, she could hardly contain her disappointment. The lesson hours dragged, and even Trey seemed less enthusiastic than usual. By the time the teenager said goodnight and headed for the bunkhouse, Lucas still hadn't appeared and Jennifer decided that he must have changed his mind.

She gathered up her books and purse, snapped off the light and walked out onto the dark porch. She was almost to the steps, when he stopped her.

"Hey." His deep voice was a low murmur in the night, his fingers closing gently but firmly around her wrist to tug her around to face him. "Where are you going?"

"Lucas!" Relief and pleased delight shimmered in her voice, easing the worry squeezing her heart. She let him take the books and purse from her arms and drop them onto a wooden chair seat before indignation claimed her. He wrapped his arms around her and pulled her close, but she stopped him with her palms braced against his chest. "Wait a minute, cowboy. First, you'd better explain why you've treated me like your aunt Matilda all night."

"I don't have an aunt Matilda," he said and tried to close the distance between them.

Jennifer refused to budge. "You know what I mean, Lucas—what's going on?"

He sighed and allowed her the small distance.

"This is the first time we've been alone all night—did you want me to walk into the house and grab you in front of Josh and Murphy? Or Charlie and Trey?"

"Well, no," Jennifer admitted. "But you might have given me some indication that you hadn't gone back to hating me."

Startled, Lucas leaned back to peer down into her face. "Hating you? Honey, I've never hated you."

"Well, you certainly didn't like me very much when we first met."

Lucas laughed, a deep amused chuckle that rumbled his chest under Jennifer's fingers. "I had a bad case of lust at first sight and it irritated the hell out of me, but that's a long way from hate."

"Oh." Mollified, she tilted her head and looked up at him. "I thought you were trouble the first time I saw you, too."

"Oh, yeah?" He smiled briefly. With a swiftness that had Jennifer gasping, he bent and swept her up in his arms before dropping into the oak rocker with her cuddled on his lap. "I didn't *think* you were trouble, I *knew* you were, and I was right. Come here."

There weren't any preliminaries. He cradled the back of her head in one big hand and kissed her with an intense, hot thoroughness that left her breathless.

When he finally lifted his mouth from hers, Jennifer was shaking. She dropped her head to his shoulder, only then realizing that her arms were wrapped tightly around his neck, her fingers smoothing in unconscious, soothing movements against his nape.

"I love that," he murmured against her temple, his voice unsteady in her ear.

"What?" she breathed, certain that he meant their shared kiss.

"Your hands on me," he said softly. "I love the way you keep touching me."

Jennifer's heart caught and Annabel's description of his childhood came back with vivid clarity. She couldn't help wondering how many loving touches the little boy had ever received, and if this passionate man Lucas kept hidden beneath his gruff, hard exterior craved the love he'd never had.

She tipped her head back and looked up into his eyes. "I love having you touch me, too, Lucas."

His body went still, his fingers tightening and closing into a fist in her hair.

"You shouldn't say things like that if you don't mean them."

His voice was rusty, barely recognizable. Jennifer felt the tense, waiting stillness in the length of his body beneath hers. In that moment, she knew with certainty that Lucas Hightower was nothing like any of the men she'd ever known, not any of her three stepfathers, nor any of the men she'd briefly dated. In all the ways that counted, she truly could trust him.

Her lips trembled in a smile and she gently traced a forefinger over the line of his forehead and down the length of his nose to his mouth.

"Oh, I mean it," she murmured. She slipped her arms around his neck and tugged him closer. "I definitely mean it."

Lucas obeyed her urging and found her mouth with his. His hand left her hair and moved to the tiny buttons that fastened the front of her dress from below her collarbone to above her knees.

He flicked open three buttons, his mouth raised a breath away from hers. "The first time I ever saw you in this dress, I thought about doing this."

Jennifer blinked drowsily, a tiny frown of concentration veeing her eyebrows. "That was over a month ago—you've thought about undressing me for a month?"

Lucas laughed softly, his breath ghosting over her lips. "I've thought about undressing you since I walked by your classroom and saw you for the first time."

"Goodness," Jennifer breathed. Her ability to concentrate was being seriously undermined by the warm brush of the back of his fingers against the inner swell of her breasts as he unbuttoned her dress.

"How do I unfasten this?" Lucas asked quietly, fingering the lace of her bra.

"There's a hook in the front, just under your hand, but...Lucas!" Her fingers stopped his just as he flicked open the hook and the lacy edges of her bra fell free.

"It's all right," he said soothingly. "Josh left an hour ago for a cattle auction in Miles City, and everyone else is sound asleep."

"Are you sure?"

"I'm sure. Trust me, honey, I wouldn't do anything to embarrass you. I know exactly how tough it is to live with a bad reputation. I'm not about to endanger yours."

Reassured, Jennifer rested her head against his shoulder, tilting her face up to brush a kiss against the underside of his jaw. He slipped his hand inside the loosened dress and stroked the soft skin of her midriff. Her pulse sped, faster and faster, and she held her breath as the callused roughness of his hand moved slowly upward, until his fingers brushed the lower curve of her breast. She gasped and shifted against him in a wordless plea and his hard fingers closed with exquisite gentleness over her breast.

"Oh, Lucas," she breathed and looked up to find his face taut with desire, the skin stretched tight over the hard thrust of his cheekbones, his eyes hot as he followed the movements of his hand against the paler skin of her breast.

The night pulsed around them, his breathing harsh, hers broken as he stroked and caressed her. His lashes flicked up and he read the total, intense, sensual abandon on her face. The need to bury himself in her was overwhelming and went beyond the driving need for sexual completion; it felt uneasily like a much more basic need to mate, possess and claim.

His hand trembled when he forced his fingers to leave the silky skin and fasten her bra.

The hook was impossible to close with one hand and, reluctant as he was to let her go, he moved her upright on his lap and used both hands to fumble the hook into the tiny metal eye.

"Lucas?" Jennifer didn't want him to stop, but the look on his face was so serious and determined, she was afraid something was wrong.

He fastened the little buttons on her dress and eased her back against his shoulder, wrapping her tightly against him with both arms. "Shh." He pressed a kiss against her temple. "If I didn't stop now, I'm not sure I could have stopped at all."

"Oh." Jennifer was vividly aware of the hard evidence of his desire under her hip. "Do you want me to leave?"

"No." His arms tightened to hold her in place. "Let me hold you for a while—talk to me."

"All right." She settled comfortably against his chest, his heartbeat pounding like a drum beneath her ear. "What about?"

"Anything—tell me about Seattle."

They sat for hours on the old porch, with Jennifer cradled on Lucas's lap. They exchanged bits and pieces of their lives, laughing at shared tales of youthful follies, until the moon came up and turned the yard lot into silvery near-daylight.

"I suppose I should go home," she said reluctantly.

"You could always stay the night." He tipped his head back and looked down at her. "There's lots of room in my bed."

"I doubt it—not as big as you are. I bet you sleep crosswise and take all the covers," she teased.

"If you'll stay, I promise you can have all the blankets, cross my heart," he said solemnly.

"If I stayed, we wouldn't need blankets," she said dryly.

"You're right," he said huskily. "We'd probably burn down the damn house." Reluctantly, he lifted her off his lap and set her upright on the porch floor. "You're a hard-hearted woman, Teacher."

"I thought we agreed to your high-school rule?" She tucked her arm around his waist and tugged him toward the steps.

He halted her, picked up her forgotten books and purse and slung his free arm over her shoulder, fitting her snugly against his side. "True, but I've been thinking—we ought to renegotiate that rule."

They stopped at her car and Lucas pulled open the door, tossing her books onto the passenger seat, and turned to wrap her close. He kissed her until she was dizzy, and when he let her go, she staggered and he caught her by the waist to steady her.

"So, what do you think?"

"About what?" She could barely think, let alone remember what he was asking her.

"The above-the-waist rule—maybe we should change it to no rules? Anything's legal?"

"I'll have to think about that." She pushed away from him and slid behind the wheel.

"Chicken," he said softly, his eyes teasing.

She didn't answer, but her frown only elicited a deep chuckle.

"I'll follow you into town to be sure you get home safe and sound."

"You don't need to drive all the way into Butte Creek," she protested, touched by his concern.

"I'm following you," he repeated, his tone brooking no argument. "Drive carefully."

The feeling of being cosseted and protected persisted down the thirty miles to Butte Creek, and after Lucas had kissed her good-night at her door. It occurred to Jennifer again that Lucas wasn't like any other man she'd ever known. Usually, she either didn't trust the man, or she made certain that she was the stronger one in the friendship.

With Lucas, it was just possible that she'd met a man who was her match.

Strangely enough, the idea wasn't at all bad.

* * *

Jennifer slept in the next morning, which made her go jogging later than usual. It was eight-thirty and already hot enough to make her glad to turn the corner of the last block for home. Mrs. Armstrong, middle-aged and friendly, was snapping the withered heads off the petunias in the bed that lined her sidewalk when Jennifer jogged past and slowed to turn into her driveway next door.

"Hi, there, dearie," the heavyset woman warbled, waving a gloved hand at her.

Jennifer jogged in place, turning in a small circle while she cooled down. "Hi, Mrs. Armstrong, how are you this morning?"

"Fine, fine, just fine." The woman tugged off her dirt-smeared gardening gloves and grinned. "But you look a little warm."

Jennifer laughed. "That's putting it mildly. I wonder how long it will take before I forget rainy, cool Seattle and get used to hot summers in Montana?"

"I told you not to go running after 7:00 a.m." The older woman shook her head at Jennifer's foolishness. "It's just too darned hot."

"It won't kill me," Jennifer insisted. "I overslept this morning and Beastie didn't want to miss his run."

The big dog's ears pricked up at his name, but he didn't get up from where he lay sprawled in the shade of the maple tree in Mrs. Armstrong's yard.

"I can't deny it surely keeps you fit and trim." Mrs. Armstrong glanced down at her own full figure in her summer sundress and then at Jennifer's long, tanned legs in white shorts.

The rumble of a truck engine sounded in the street behind them and Jennifer glanced over her shoulder, her eyes widening in surprise as she recognized Lucas's black pickup.

Mrs. Armstrong's eyes lit with interest when the truck turned into Jennifer's driveway and Lucas's tall, broad-shouldered figure stepped out. Dressed in a black Stetson, polished black boots, faded jeans and an unornamented black leather vest over a white dress shirt, he was every woman's dream of the perfect cowboy.

"Oh, my," Mrs. Armstrong whispered with excitement. "Whatever is Lucas Hightower doing here?"

Jennifer frowned at her. "He's a friend of mine."

The chatty neighbor looked taken aback. "Oh, I'm sorry, dear, I didn't know."

"Hello, Lucas," Jennifer called, smiling warmly as she walked toward him.

"Hello, Lucas," Mrs. Armstrong called from her petunia bed.

Lucas looked past Jennifer and recognized the mother of the teenager who pumped gas for him at the station he frequented. "Mornin', ma'am," he said politely, touching the brim of his Stetson.

"What are you doing in town at this hour of the day, Lucas?" Jennifer asked.

He glanced down and found her looking up at him with little worry lines creasing her forehead. He quelled the impulse to smooth them away with his forefinger and nodded toward the house.

"Why don't we go inside and I'll tell you."

Jennifer glanced across the lawn at Mrs. Armstrong. Her neighbor was industriously snipping away at her petunias, but she was obviously straining to hear their conversation.

Jennifer's eyes brimmed with amusement as they met Lucas's. "All right." She snapped her fingers at Beastie and he bounded up from his shaded, grass bed.

The house was cool and shady, the drapes drawn against the growing heat outside. Jennifer pushed the door shut behind them and turned to look at Lucas.

"What is it? Is something wrong? Is it Trey—"

"Nothing's wrong," he said hastily. "Trey's fine— sorry I worried you, honey, I just didn't want to talk in front of your neighbor."

"Oh." Jennifer sighed and relaxed, her smile mischievous as she laughed. "She is a bit of a gossip, but she's good-hearted. So, why are you here?"

"I have to leave town," he said bluntly. "Josh is supposed to be in Miles City at a cattle auction but I got a call from him this morning—he's in Great Falls and won't make it to the auction."

Jennifer blinked. Lucas was clearly upset, and she wasn't sure why. "Is he all right?" she asked cautiously.

Lucas's expression reflected irritation. "Physically, yes, he's fine, but I'm not so sure he hasn't gone completely crazy."

"This sounds serious," Jennifer commented, stepping closer to him. "What's he doing in Great Falls?"

"Somebody in Miles City told him they'd seen Sarah Drummond there."

"Oh, I see."

"Well, maybe you do, but I don't." Exasperated, Lucas lifted his Stetson, shoved impatient fingers through his hair and settled the hat back over his forehead. "This whole thing with Sarah is out of control," he said, starting to pace the room. "He's been damned near impossible to live with, not to mention that he's worrying Murphy half-sick with his fighting, drinking and hell-raising ever since she left. Now he's chasing off across Montana because of a half-baked rumor that somebody thought they saw her somewhere.''

''Maybe he's in love with her,'' Jennifer said quietly.

''Hell, how could he be in love with her?'' he demanded, glaring at her. ''He only dated her for a few months. How serious could that be?''

''I don't know, but I'm not sure it takes a long time to fall in love.''

Her quiet, thoughtful voice brought his pacing to an abrupt halt. Lucas stared at her broodingly, his expression shuttered behind half-lowered lashes.

''You may be right,'' he said slowly. Two strides of his long legs brought him to a halt in front of her. ''The real reason I stopped by was because I might be gone for a week or more. After the auction, I have to drive over to see a breeder in the Judith Basin to look at a couple of bulls we're thinking about buying.''

He reached out and curled his hand around the back of her neck. His palm was warm; his thumb brushed back and forth over the sensitive skin beneath her ear and Jennifer shivered just before he tugged her gently forward and into his arms.

''Mostly I stopped here to kiss you goodbye before I left town.''

Jennifer didn't protest when he lowered his mouth to hers; she only clenched her fingers over the edges of the black vest he was wearing and held on while her senses skyrocketed.

At last, Lucas broke the kiss and lifted his head to rest his forehead against hers. "Damn, you're good," he whispered roughly.

"So are you," she whispered back. "Skyrockets."

"Really?" He opened his eyes and watched her nod solemnly. "Good—you set off a few fireworks yourself."

"Good." She smiled blissfully when he hugged her closer, his head bent over hers.

"I have to go," he whispered with resignation.

"Are you sure?" she whispered back.

"Yeah, unfortunately." He kissed her one last time, a quick hard kiss of possession, before he released her and pulled open the door. "Don't go kissing any other guys while I'm gone," he warned.

"I won't," she promised.

He stepped out on the porch and Jennifer stood on the top step, watching as he strode to his truck, climbed in and backed out of her driveway. He answered her wave with a twist of his hand and then he was gone.

Jennifer sighed and turned back into the house, wondering what in the world she was going to do while he was gone.

Lucas had been gone for one week, three days, four hours and seventeen minutes.

Jennifer was heartily sick of counting the hours. Fortunately for her state of mind, his late-night call that woke her after midnight had confirmed that he'd be home today in time to enter the rodeo held with the county fair.

She set off for the fairground dressed in her favorite white sundress, with a floppy straw hat on her head, heart-shaped pink-framed sunglasses perched on her nose and her toes tipped in matching pink nail polish and buckled into strappy sandals.

"Jennifer! Jennifer! Up here!"

Jennifer heard her name called and searched the tiers of white-painted benches above her. An arm waved wildly and beneath it, she spotted Annabel's white hair tucked under a wide-brimmed hat. Jennifer waved back and climbed the narrow aisles, dodging laughing children.

When she finally reached Annabel, she dropped onto the bench with a sigh of relief. "Good grief, Annabel, you didn't tell me it would be this crazy."

"This is nothing," Annabel assured her. "It'll be even crazier tonight. You better save your energy— after a couple hours of this, we're meeting Rose and Jackie at the exhibit pavilion for the flower judging, then Rose has some pickles entered in the canning division and we have to go watch the judges make their decision."

Jennifer heard the names of two teachers from school who were cronies of Annabel's and groaned, laughing. "I'm not sure I'm old enough to be out with you wild women, Annabel. My feet hurt just thinking about all that walking."

"Oh, phooey," Annabel scoffed, her blue eyes twinkling. "You young people are such lightweights. I wait all year for the county fair, I'm not about to miss a minute of it."

An hour later, the opening parade was finished, the bulldogging winner announced and the crowd had thinned in the grandstands as people drifted away to sample the other offerings at the fair. Annabel decided to get them some drinks. She negotiated the steep steps and disappeared in the crowd below.

Jennifer turned her attention back to the action in the arena, where a cowboy was desperately trying to stay on the back of a fire-breathing Brahma bull for eight long seconds.

"Excuse me? Miss McCleary—Jennifer Mc-Cleary?"

The tentative voice at her elbow brought Jennifer's gaze around. She looked up into the face of an attractive woman in her mid-thirties. She had coffee-brown hair, thick-lashed blue eyes and a figure that stopped just short of being plump.

"Yes?"

"I'm Suzie Webber, Trey's mother. I wonder if I can have a few words with you?"

Chapter Nine

Jennifer was nonplussed for a moment, but she quickly recovered, caught up the full skirt of her dress and slid over to make room on the bench beside her.

"Of course, please—sit down."

"Thanks." Trey's mother perched on the edge of the bench, fidgeting nervously with the trio of silver Mexican bracelets on her wrist.

"It's nice to finally meet you," Jennifer offered when the woman continued to glance nervously about her. "You have a very intelligent young son, Mrs. Webber. I have great hopes for him."

"He is smart, isn't he?" A smile bloomed across the woman's face, her eyes brightening as she met Jennifer's gaze. Suzie's smile relieved the tense, drawn lines of her face, making her seem years younger.

"Yes, very much so," Jennifer said gently. "He's doing well in his studies this summer."

"Is he?" Suzie leaned forward, resting her palms against her jeans-clad thighs. Her fingertips dug into the fabric, making little indentations against the denim. "I was hoping he'd behave himself and study—he likes you a lot—but I haven't seen him since school let out and I was worrying, you know?"

"He's doing very well—in fact, better than I had hoped. He'll not only move on with his classmates this fall, but if he continues working as hard during the coming school year, he'll give Butte Creek's top students a lot of competition."

Suzie heaved a sigh of relief and visibly relaxed. "That's wonderful. He did so well in school when he was a little guy, but when he was about twelve, he just seemed to stop caring about schoolwork."

"That happens with some children," Jennifer agreed diplomatically. "But Trey is a young man with a great deal of potential and I think that he's become more committed to his studies this summer. Not only is he doing well in his core subjects of English, math and history, but he's asked to take on additional work to learn basic computer skills."

"He has?" Suzie was obviously surprised. "I can't even get him to pick up his room at home, let alone volunteer for extra work."

"Well, he's working very hard—not only with his schoolwork, but on the job, as well. Lucas says that what he lacks in experience, he more than makes up in his willingness to learn how to do a task and do it right."

At the mention of Lucas's name, Suzie visibly stiffened. Her back grew poker-straight and her blue eyes glittered in a face gone pale except for a brush of hectic color over her cheekbones.

"Lucas!" she said with loathing, her face twisted with anger. "Lucas Hightower knows absolutely nothing about doing anything right! How could he possibly know if *my* son is doing something right? That man should never be allowed near a child, especially my child—mine and Clay's!"

She was crying now, tears running down her face, streaking black mascara stripes over her cheeks.

"Mrs. Webber, please." Jennifer was aghast. She'd known from Annabel's brief comments that Trey's mother felt strongly about Lucas, but the depth of bitter anguish in the woman's outburst shocked her. She looked quickly around them, but the crowd had thinned and they were alone in this small section of the grandstand. "Trey seems to like Lucas," she said reassuringly, fumbling in her pocket for a tissue to give to Suzie. "And I see them nearly every evening. I'm sure Trey would tell me if he wasn't being treated well by any of the men at the Lazy H."

"You don't understand." Suzie used the tissue to wipe her eyes and face. She not only wiped away her tears, but also the makeup that had covered the shadowy circles under her eyes and the rouge that had added color to the sallow paleness of her cheeks. "Nobody understands." She fixed Jennifer with a baleful look. "I suppose Lucas has given you an earful about what a terrible person I am—and Trey, too, no doubt. I'm sure that's why he hasn't called since he went to work at that place!" She spat the last words, her blue eyes slitted accusingly.

"Mrs. Webber, I don't know what you think Lucas told me, but he hasn't said anything bad about you. In fact," Jennifer added, "I've never heard him say anything about you at all."

Suzie's blue gaze searched Jennifer's for a long, tense moment before she looked away, fumbling in her purse for something.

"Give him time," she muttered, her dark brown hair swinging forward to hide her face as she bent over to continue her search in the bag at her feet. "He will."

"I'm sorry, I didn't catch that." Jennifer leaned forward. "What did you—"

"I'm back," Annabel called from three steps below them on the grandstand aisle. She slid onto the bench beside Suzie. "Whew," she said, smiling pleasantly. "It surely is hot out, isn't it? I'm glad I decided to get a large drink instead of a small one. Would you like a sip of lemonade?" She held out the moisture-dotted plastic cup toward Suzie, who shook her head sullenly, and then to Jennifer, who also declined. "It's nice to see you, Suzie. Has Jennifer been telling you how well Trey's doing in his studies?"

"Yes." Suzie had found a pack of cigarettes in her bag and tapped one out before snapping open a silver lighter. She lit the cigarette with trembling fingers and took a deep breath, exhaling a cloud of smoke before returning the lighter and the half-empty pack of cigarettes to her purse. "She says Trey's doing just great. But then, that's what you hoped, isn't it?" she asked resentfully. "That Trey would do better without me?"

"No, that's not what I thought at all," Annabel said reasonably. "In fact, I think Trey would do far better with you in his life. Children need their parents. But Trey needs a mother who's healthy, and that's something you aren't going to be until you stop drinking."

"I can stop anytime I want," Suzie snapped.

"Then prove it and stop now," Annabel said implacably.

"I will—I am." Suzie glared at the little white-haired woman. "But not because you threatened to report me to the cops and the welfare board for giving alcohol to a minor, Annabel Fitch. I don't want Trey taken away permanently—I want him home again. I'm checking into an inpatient treatment center in Glasgow this afternoon. I only came here to talk to Trey's teacher before I left, just to make sure he's doing okay."

"That's wonderful, Mrs. Webber." Jennifer's smile held heartfelt relief.

"I'm holding you responsible, Miss McCleary," Suzie said, her voice shaking with half threat, half plea, "if Lucas does anything to hurt Trey."

"Lucas would never knowingly harm your son," Jennifer assured her.

Suzie's face twisted, her blue eyes darkening. "That's where you're wrong. He might not hurt Trey if he were just any boy, but the fact that he's my son is a strike against him."

Jennifer shook her head in denial, but she didn't know what to say in response to the woman's clear conviction that Lucas harbored enough dislike for her to hurt an innocent boy.

"How are you getting to Glasgow, Suzie?" Annabel asked.

"Ed Pyle is driving me," she said, bending over to collect her purse.

"Hmm." Annabel eyed her, gave a determined nod and stood. "I'll drive you. We both know that Ed won't make it ten miles down the road without stopping for a drink. If you've truly made up your mind to go into treatment, there's no sense throwing stumbling blocks in your way."

Suzie frowned up at her, hesitated and then stood. "All right. Thanks, Mrs. Fitch. You're probably right about Ed." She turned and held out her hand to Jennifer. "Thanks, Miss McCleary. I really appreciate everything you're doing for Trey, teaching him this summer and all." She grimaced, scrubbed a hand over her cheeks and shrugged. "Sorry I got so emotional."

"That's all right." Jennifer took her hand in a warm grip. "Good luck."

"Thanks."

Annabel stepped back and let Suzie precede her into the aisle.

"I'm sorry I won't be here to tour the fair with you, Jennifer," she said hurriedly, glancing quickly after Suzie, who was moving down the steps. "But I've been trying to convince Suzie to enter treatment for a long time. I just can't afford to miss the opportunity—one has to strike while the iron's hot, you know."

"Of course, don't worry about me."

Annabel thrust her large cup of lemonade into Jennifer's hand and bustled after Suzie.

Jennifer saw Annabel's spare figure hurry down the steps and catch up with Suzie, then watched the two women disappear through the exit.

A roar from the crowd drew her attention back to the arena below. Jennifer sipped Annabel's lemonade and fanned herself with the wide-brimmed straw hat. The afternoon grew later and the crowd in the grandstand ebbed and flowed.

"Hey, Miss McCleary!"

Jennifer's gaze left the dusty arena below where a cowboy was trying to rope an uncooperative calf and found Trey amid a group of laughing, noisy teenagers at the entrance to the grandstand. She smiled and waved a hello, and Trey bent to whisper in the ear of a girl next to him. The girl nodded and the two left the group to climb up the steps to Jennifer.

"Hello, Trey." She recognized the blond girl with him and smiled warmly. "And Cindy—how nice to see you."

"Do you mind if we sit with you?" Trey asked.

"Not at all." Jennifer slid over to make room for the two. Trey stood back and courteously seated Cindy first before he dropped onto the bench and stretched out his long legs in front of him. "Are you two enjoying the fair?"

"Yes, we're having a terrific time," Cindy said happily, glancing shyly at Trey.

"It's great," Trey concurred. "But the rodeo is always the best part. Have Lucas and Josh ridden yet?"

Jennifer's heart skipped a beat. "No," she managed to say casually. "Are they going to? I wasn't sure if Lucas was back in town."

"Yeah, he's here—he just got to the fairground about fifteen minutes ago. We were back of the chutes with Murphy and Charlie and he asked us to see if we could find you. He would have come himself, but he and Josh are team roping."

"When?" Jennifer asked.

"Any minute now. Lucas said to bring you down to the chutes as soon as they're done. Have you ever seen team roping, Miss McCleary?"

"No, I haven't." Jennifer looked back at the arena where yet another cowboy was flying through the air while the horse he'd struggled to stay astride kicked and bucked his way in the opposite direction. "Is it dangerous?"

"No, team roping isn't dangerous at all—unless you get unlucky and fall off your horse." Trey grinned at Cindy, who rolled her eyes in disgust. He proceeded to give Jennifer a quick rundown of the sport.

"It sounds fairly simple," Jennifer said when he was through.

"Simple, but hard as h—uh, heck to do." Trey shook his head. "I've watched Lucas and Josh practicing and even Josh misses sometimes."

"Mmm," Jennifer acknowledged. The teenagers chatted enthusiastically and somehow she managed to respond, but Jennifer's gaze was busy searching the far side of the arena. Cowboys milled behind the gates, some perched on the top railing of the fence, some atop horses, but she didn't recognize Lucas in the ceaseless activity.

"I think they're up next," Trey commented. He reached across Cindy and caught Jennifer's arm to get her attention. "Over there, Miss McCleary."

Just then Lucas's and Josh's names were called over the loudspeaker.

"And three-time champion team ropers, a pair of brothers from our own county, Lucas and Josh Hightower, ladies and gentlemen."

The gate flew open and a steer exploded out of the pen, followed by two riders. With a fluidity and precision that was a sheer pleasure to watch, Josh and Lucas swung ropes in near unison, Josh's loop settling smoothly over the steer's horns while Lucas deftly snared the back feet. Within seconds after leaving the gate, the steer was unable to move, stretched with taut ropes between the two men and their horses. The buzzer went off and the crowd roared its appreciation. Lucas kneed his horse closer, slackening the rope enough to let him shake the loop loose, and the steer bounded away just as Josh shook his rope free from its horns.

Jennifer was mesmerized. Unfortunately, it was over so quickly she barely had time to register all the details.

"And that time is going to be hard to beat, ladies and gentlemen! Let's hear it for the Hightowers!"

The crowd roared as Lucas and Josh touched their hats in acknowledgment and rode out of the arena.

"Come on." Trey stood and stepped into the aisle. "Let's go down and congratulate them."

The area behind the chutes leading into the arena was crowded with cowboys and horses, pickup trucks were backed up with their beds facing the fence, creating an uneven, dusty alleyway between the arena and the open prairie beyond the fairground.

Jennifer nearly ran to keep up with Trey's long strides as he threaded in and out of the throng. She dodged a cowboy with a saddle slung over his shoulder and nearly lost her hat. She grabbed it and tugged it off, clutching the straw brim in one hand while she hurried to catch up with Trey and Cindy. Finally, Jennifer saw Murphy's familiar bowlegged figure, and Josh beside him. Lucas stood to one side, half-turned away from her, his head bent as he listened to Murphy.

Jennifer stopped walking, frozen in place as she stared at him. He was wearing the familiar black Stetson, tugged low over his forehead, a white pearl-snapped shirt, blue jeans, black boots and dark brown leather chaps.

Josh looked up and saw her. Jennifer knew that he reached out and touched Lucas's arm, nodding in her direction, but all her attention was focused on Lucas. He glanced around quickly, a smile breaking across his stern features when his searching gaze found her.

The noise of the crowd faded and all she could see was Lucas. The stretch of the white cotton over the strength of his shoulders, the splash of the sunlight across his cheek and jaw beneath the brim of his hat, the solid height and breadth of his big body—all of him, everything about him, was unbearably dear.

Oh, no. The truth hit her with staggering, heart-stopping force. *I'm in love with him.*

He took a step toward her.

"Winners are the roping team of Lucas and Josh Hightower!"

The noise from the crowd was deafening. Murphy slapped Lucas on the back, Trey let out a war whoop and swung Cindy in a circle. Lucas's face lit with a wide grin and he held out his arms.

Jennifer didn't know she ran. She only knew that Lucas caught her when she threw herself into his arms. Hands at her waist, he swung her up until she laughed down at him before he lowered her into a bone-crushing hug.

"Congratulations!" Her arms were wrapped around his neck, her feet dangling in the air a good six inches off the ground. "You won!"

Lucas tilted his head back to look at her. "Yup, we did." He bent forward, his lips at her ear. "Damn, I missed you."

The low, fervently growled words sent shivers over her. She tipped her head back, searching the warm, unguarded depths of his blue eyes.

"I missed you, too."

His arms tightened and his head dipped toward her. Just when Jennifer's lashes were drifting lower, her bones beginning to melt, Murphy's voice jolted them back to reality.

"Hey, you two, we're goin' to go get something to eat—you comin'?"

Lucas's hot blue stare met Jennifer's for one searing moment before his arms loosened and he carefully set her back on her feet.

"Yeah, Murphy, we're coming." He unbuckled his chaps and quickly stripped them off, tossing them into the bed of his pickup with the saddles, blankets and bridles. He slid an arm around Jennifer's waist, his gaze sharpening over her features. "You all right?" he asked, one hand lifting to gently tuck a strand of hair behind her ear.

"Fine, just fine." Jennifer knew her smile wobbled, but Lucas seemed to accept her assurances.

"Hurry up, you two," Murphy yelled over his shoulder. "I'm hungry enough to eat a bear."

"We're coming," Lucas yelled back. "All that old codger ever thinks about is his stomach," he complained, his eyes twinkling.

"And poker," Jennifer reminded him.

"And poker," Lucas agreed. "It's a good thing the fair doesn't have a category for poker playing or before the night's over, Murphy would be in jail for cheating."

The mouth-watering smell of barbecued beef and pork reached them long before they neared the big tent with its long rows of tables and metal folding chairs. Murphy, Trey and Cindy were almost through the line, plates loaded, when Lucas and Jennifer stepped inside. Fortunately, the line of diners moved quickly, and the three were barely making inroads on barbecued ribs when Lucas and Jennifer joined them.

Jennifer dropped into her chair. "Murphy, does this taste as good as it smells?"

"Better," he answered succinctly, grinning at her. He made a halfhearted pass with a napkin at barbecue sauce smudged at the corner of his mouth before picking up another rib.

Lucas shook out a paper napkin from the stack he'd dropped on the table and turned Jennifer to face him. "There's only one way to do this." Carefully, he tucked the top edges of the napkin inside the scoop neckline of her dress. The back of his fingers brushed against the soft beginning swell of her breasts but he didn't look up; instead, he meticulously straightened the white paper and spread another white square over her lap. He handed her yet a third napkin before he met her gaze. "You have to eat ribs with your fingers, and if we don't cover you up, you're going to get barbecue sauce all over that pretty white dress."

The heat in his eyes trapped her breath in her lungs before he turned to his own plate, releasing her.

She picked up a rib and began to eat, but it was several moments before she was breathing normally and actually tasted what she was eating.

"What happened to Josh and Charlie?" she asked, realizing that their group was two people short. "Aren't they joining us?"

"They're taking the horses over to the barns," Lucas told her. "Soon as they're done, they'll be here. Neither of them would miss eating barbecue."

Jennifer flicked a glance at the three across the table. Murphy was listening to a white-haired rancher on his left and Trey was whispering in Cindy's ear. "Is Josh all right? Did he find what he was looking for in Great Falls?" she asked quietly.

Lucas's eyes turned bleak. "No, he didn't."

"I'm sorry," Jennifer said. "Is he terribly upset?"

"You might say that." Lucas tossed a stripped rib bone on his plate and grimaced. "It's liable to be a rough night."

Instinctively, Jennifer reached out to touch him, realizing too late that her fingers were sticky with barbecue sauce.

"Oops." She lifted her hand away from his bare forearm, leaving five brownish-red fingerprint smudges.

Lucas's tense face relaxed into a grin and he shook his head at her. "I guess I should have covered me with napkins, too."

"Sorry." She grabbed a clean napkin and scrubbed at his arm. "If I'd known I was dangerous, I'd have sat farther away."

"Hey, Trey."

The youthful voice interrupted Lucas's reply. A group of teenagers, three boys and two girls, entered the tent and gathered behind Trey and Cindy.

"Hi, Miss McCleary." Chris Jamison, a tall, lanky sophomore who had been a student of Jennifer's, gave her a wide grin that exposed teeth highlighted by silver braces.

"Hello, Chris," Jennifer replied, smiling a greeting as the group echoed an enthusiastic hello.

"We're going over to the pavilion to listen to the live music," Chris said to Trey. "Why don't you and Cindy come along?"

"I don't know, Chris." Trey glanced at Cindy before his gaze shifted to Lucas.

"Aw, come on," Marty Granson, a fresh-faced brunette with her own set of braces, cajoled. "Cindy wants to, don't you, Cindy?"

"It might be fun, Trey."

"I have to catch a ride home with Murphy," Trey said firmly, his gaze shifting to the older man. "What time are you leaving? Do you want me to meet you in the parking lot? Or back here?"

"I'll take you home, Trey," Chris interjected. "I've got my dad's car and I have to give Marty a lift."

"No," Trey rejected the offer instantly. "I'm going home with Murphy—I have to work tomorrow." He turned back to Murphy.

"You can meet me at my truck in the parking lot at midnight," Murphy drawled, his keen eyes approving as they met Trey's. "That should give me time enough to take a turn around the dance floor with all the pretty girls and tell a few lies."

Trey grinned at him, shoved back his chair and stood up.

"See you at midnight," he said, holding Cindy's chair while she stood. "Good night, Miss McCleary, Lucas."

"Good night," Lucas said casually.

"Good night, have fun. Be careful."

"We will," Cindy answered, tucking her arm through Trey's. "Bye."

Jennifer watched the laughing group of teenagers leave the tent. "I'm worried about this," she said aloud, her forehead furrowing in a frown.

"Why is that?"

She glanced at Lucas to find both him and Murphy sipping their coffee, watching her with identical looks of curiosity on their faces.

"Because Chris and both of the boys with him have been in trouble at school and with their parents. Granted, it's been minor sorts of mischief, but Trey has been doing so well. I don't want him to get into any more trouble."

"Let it go, Jennifer," Lucas advised. "You can't wrap Trey in cotton and guard him all the time. He has to live in the world and survive—he has to be responsible for his own life. You can't do it for him."

"He's right," Murphy agreed. "Besides, I think Trey learned his lesson. He'll be at the truck to meet me at midnight, don't worry."

"I hope so." Jennifer wasn't convinced.

"What isn't she supposed to worry about?"

Josh dragged out the chair beside her and sat down, settling a plate loaded with a staggering amount of food on the table in front of him.

"Trey," Murphy replied. "The woman worries too much about that kid."

"We all worry about the kid," Charlie put in. He'd taken the chair on the far side of Josh and leaned forward to smile at Jennifer. "But he's gonna do all right. He's got a good heart."

"Yup, he does that," Murphy agreed.

"Josh, did you get the horses settled with no problem?" Lucas asked.

"Sure," Josh swallowed and pointed his fork at Lucas. "I'm telling you, we ought to go down the road this summer. Our time this afternoon damn near beat the record."

"Been there, done that," Lucas replied succinctly. "I've got no itch to follow the rodeo circuit again. I like being home every night and sleeping in my own bed."

Jennifer sipped her coffee and listened to the four men discuss the winning rides in the afternoon rodeo. It wasn't only Trey who worried her. There was a raw edge to Josh tonight; a restless, brooding pain glittered in his eyes and hovered about him in a dangerous dark aura.

Charlie and Josh ate while the others drank their coffee. When the last rib was picked clean and tossed on the plate with its companions, Josh pushed back his chair and stood.

"I'm outta here," he announced.

"Where are you going?" Lucas asked.

"Down to the Wild Horse Saloon. I told Colby I'd meet him down there after I ate."

"Why don't you come over to the hall with us," Murphy suggested. "There's a good live band, and all the cake and pie you can eat for the price of admission."

"Maybe later." Josh settled his hat over his forehead, picked up his trash, nodded goodbye to Jennifer and stalked off.

Murphy sighed heavily, the sound breaking the silence at the table. "There's gonna be trouble tonight, I can feel it in my bones."

"Yep, so can I." Charlie stood and collected his own used plate and utensils. "Reckon I better trail along after him. Not that I stand much chance of keepin' him out of trouble, but at least I can haul him home afterward.''

''Well.'' Murphy slapped his palms on the table and pushed himself upright. ''I hope you two aren't going to let me down.''

''No, we're coming.'' Lucas glanced down at Jennifer. ''Ready to get your toes stepped on?''

''By you?''

''Hell, no, not by me!'' He looked insulted. ''By Murphy.''

''Now, that's a lie,'' Murphy denied indignantly. ''I can dance rings around you, boy, and I ain't never stepped on a woman's toes in my life. Besides, I know for a fact that you haven't danced with a woman for at least fifteen years!''

He continued to argue with Lucas as the trio left the tent and worked their way across the neon-lit fairground to the community hall.

''Murphy! How nice to see you.'' The slender woman behind the ticket counter smiled with delight, her cheeks blushing a becoming pink.

''Evening, Wanda.'' Murphy smiled with equal appreciation.

Lucas bent over, his lips brushing Jennifer's ear. ''Wanda's been sweet on Murphy for the last twenty years.''

Jennifer's eyes twinkled and she struggled to keep from laughing.

''And Lucas! What a nice surprise.'' Wanda's mouth dropped open and she stared at Lucas's hand resting on Jennifer's waist for one long, speechless moment before she recovered her composure. ''And you've brought our new teacher with you.''

"Yes, I have," Lucas said evenly. He looked at Jennifer. "Have you met Wanda, Jennifer? No? Well, I don't know how you missed her. Wanda owns the beauty shop here in town."

"It's nice to meet you." Jennifer smiled and held out her hand to be stamped on the back with a red rose.

Wanda took their money, stamped the back of their hands and would have kept Murphy with her to chat, but a large group of people descended on her counter and she reluctantly released Murphy's hand and let them move on.

"Murphy, when are you going to marry that woman and put her out of her misery?" Lucas demanded mildly.

"Hell, if I married every woman who looked kindly on me, I'd be a bigamist a dozen times over."

Inside the hall, a six-piece band played on a stage against one wall, their lively music filling the huge room. Couples dipped and swayed on the polished wooden floor, while nondancers stood around the perimeter, laughing and talking, or waited six and eight bodies deep around the refreshment table.

"I'm claimin' the first dance, Jennifer," Murphy declared. "After that, I'll turn you over to Lucas. Course, he's so darn selfish he probably won't let me dance with you twice."

"You're probably right," Lucas said easily.

Murphy tucked Jennifer's hand into the crook of his arm and led her into the crowd. As he swung her around the floor, she saw Lucas back up against a wall, cross his arms and wait patiently, his gaze following them around the room.

When the song ended and Murphy returned her, she was laughing and slightly breathless.

"Here she is, Lucas, safe and sound." Murphy bent and brushed a quick kiss against her cheek before looking at Lucas. "The girl can dance—see that you don't step on her feet."

"Right," Lucas drawled, claiming Jennifer's hand in his bigger, warm palm. "You just be sure you don't make a habit of kissing her."

Murphy laughed, waggled his eyebrows suggestively at Jennifer and took himself off to the refreshment table.

"Has Murphy ever been married?" Jennifer asked as Lucas led her across the floor to the shadowy far side. Two old-fashioned, mirrored globes hung from the ceiling, spinning slowly and throwing out glittering diamonds of colored light to spangle the wooden floor.

"No." Lucas turned her into his arms and slid her hands around his neck before resting his on her waist. "He told me that he came close once, but something happened and it didn't work out."

"It's odd." She tucked her head against his shoulder, her lips brushing his throat when she spoke. "He's a man who truly enjoys women, I would have thought he would have chosen to marry."

"I think he wanted to—it was just never the right time, the right place, the right woman."

Jennifer shivered. "It's such a roll of the dice, isn't it? Being in the right place, at the right time... Do you suppose that's what happened with Josh and Sarah?"

Lucas sighed heavily, his chest rising and falling beneath her breasts. "I don't know what happened. He won't talk about it, except to say that she left town without telling him why. I think that's part of what's driving him so crazy. He doesn't know why she left him."

"Did he tell you what happened in Great Falls?"

"There wasn't much to tell. A friend claimed he'd seen Sarah working at a department store there, but Josh spent days searching and never found her. Enough about my brother—what did you do while I was gone?"

"Took Beastie running, read a book about the Civil War, went to a movie with Annabel and spent nearly every night at the Lazy H."

Lucas frowned. "You didn't miss me at all, did you?"

"Of course I did. What did you do?"

"I spent my days in an auction barn that smelled like cattle, horses and manure, and my nights in a lonely motel room watching movies on cable TV. Bad movies," he added with a grimace of disgust. "Then I drove over to the Judith Basin and bought a bull."

"It sounds to me like your life was just about as dull as mine while you were gone," she teased, running the tip of a forefinger down his cheek.

"I could have gone downstairs to the bar and picked up a redhead that smiled at me during dinner," he commented, his gaze intent on hers.

Jennifer stiffened and pushed away from him. "Strange women were trying to pick you up at dinner?" she demanded.

Lucas smiled, his hands tightening on her waist to keep her from shoving away from him even more.

"Would you have minded?"

"Would you have minded if I picked up a strange cowboy while you were gone?" she countered, frowning at him.

"Hell, yes," he growled. He stared into her flushed face, his fingers moving in soothing circles against her waist. "Let's get out of here."

He tugged her hands down from around his neck, threaded her fingers through his and pulled her with him out a side door.

The door whooshed shut behind them. Jennifer barely had time to register the sudden quiet darkness of the night, before Lucas crowded her against the outer wall.

Chapter Ten

"Lucas," Jennifer whispered just before his mouth closed over hers. She was trapped between the wall behind her and the warm, hard wall of his body in front of her. She pressed closer and was rewarded by the instant, responsive shudder of his big body against hers.

When he lifted his head at last, his breathing was harsh, his heartbeat hammering inside his chest. He nuzzled warm lips beneath her ear and down the curve of her throat before he found the racing pulse at the base of her neck.

"You make me crazy," he murmured, his voice a throaty rasp.

Jennifer smiled mistily, her fingers flexing against the thick silk of his hair. He muttered something unintelligible and trailed his lips up the underside of her jaw, one hand cradling her head in one palm to tilt her face up. He brushed hot, tasting kisses over her chin, cheek, the corner of her forehead, and her lowered lashes, until she was breathless with wanting.

"Lucas!"

The door crashed open behind them. Startled, Jennifer clutched Lucas's shoulders and stared with round-eyed shock at Murphy and Charlie.

"What?" Lucas snarled, instinctively shifting Jennifer closer to the wall, his body shielding her from the shaft of light that fell through the open door and across the far end of the concrete steps where they stood.

"Damn." Murphy caught a glimpse of Jennifer's mussed hair and reddened lips and swore aloud. "I'm sorry, boy, but Josh is in trouble. I wouldn't have bothered you, but this can't wait."

"Where is he?" Lucas asked.

"Over at the saloon," Charlie said. "Zach Colby's tryin' to keep him from gettin' killed, but he's hell-bent on findin' trouble, Lucas, and I figured I better come and get you."

Lucas bit off a curse. "That's all right, Charlie." He glanced down at Jennifer, then back at the men. "Give us a minute, okay? I'll be right there."

"Sure, Lucas."

"Damn, I'm sorry, honey," Lucas's eyes held regret and he caught her against him, dropping his cheek against the silky crown of her head. "I have to go. When Josh gets like this, there's no telling what kind of trouble he can get into."

"Don't worry about me." Jennifer hugged him, her face tucked against his throat. "Josh needs you."

Wordlessly, he returned her hug with a strength that left her breathless, brushed a last kiss across her lips and stepped back. Then they walked over to Murphy and Charlie.

"Murphy, would you take Jennifer home? Charlie and I will go get Josh."

"Oh, no, you don't," Jennifer said adamantly. "I'm going with you."

"No, you're not." Lucas's hard voice brooked no argument. "Ten to one, Josh is slugging everybody who gets within three feet of him. I'm not taking you into a barroom brawl."

"Now you listen to me, Lucas Hightower." Jennifer tilted her chin, her eyes daring him to argue with her. "I've taken knives and guns away from sixteen-year-old boys who've outweighed me by a hundred pounds. I'm not about to be sent home to wait and wring my hands while I go crazy worrying about whether you're all right."

Lucas glared at her, but she didn't back down.

"Let her come along, boss," Charlie said. "I'll watch out for her."

"All right, you can come," Lucas said through his teeth. "But you stay with Charlie and neither of you takes more than two steps inside the door."

"Sure, Lucas," Charlie answered.

Jennifer nodded in agreement. Lucas turned on his heel and strode away, Murphy on his heels. Charlie slowed his steps for Jennifer, but she walked faster, nearly running, and they quickly caught up to the two men.

The Wild Horse Saloon was only six blocks away, but Jennifer was out of breath when they reached it. Lucas stopped dead still with his hand on the door-knob and looked back at her.

"Don't forget, two steps inside the door—and you stick to Charlie like you're glued to him."

"Yes, sir," she snapped.

He glared at her again and yanked open the door. Raucous music, accompanied by yells and shouts, poured out onto the sidewalk, along with a cloud of cigarette smoke and the yeasty smell of beer. He stepped over the threshold, Murphy at his side, and stopped abruptly.

"Dammit!"

Jennifer peered around his biceps, her eyes widening as she took in the pandemonium. Josh was standing in the center of the room, back-to-back with a tall blond man. Around them, men were fighting in twos, threes and sometimes fours, while they crashed into one another and turned furniture into splintered chunks of wood. Even as she watched, one of the two men Josh was holding off landed a blow to his chin and his head snapped back. He staggered backward into the blond man, who glanced over his shoulder, saw Josh was still standing and turned back to the three men he was fighting.

"My goodness," she breathed, eyes round.

Lucas glanced at her. "Now aren't you glad you came?" he growled.

"Hey, Lucas!"

He snapped his head back around. The bartender was waving frantically at him from behind the bar.

"Get your brother outta here! He's wrecking my place!" the man yelled.

"Yeah, yeah." Lucas glanced at Murphy. "You ready?"

"Yup." Murphy spit on his hands, rubbed them together and followed Lucas into the fray.

Lucas moved through the battling crowd, shouldering and tossing men aside in his wake, while Murphy guarded his back. He reached Josh and Zach Colby, tapped Josh on the shoulder and ducked instantly, dodging the swift, instinctive punch Josh threw.

Jennifer gasped. If Lucas hadn't ducked, Josh's fist would have connected with his chin.

"He's good, ain't he?" Charlie said admiringly.

"Which one?" she said, staring at the two brothers. Although she couldn't hear them over the noise, Lucas was clearly insisting Josh leave the bar. Josh was just as clearly refusing. Even from this distance, Jennifer could see the reckless, wild light in Josh's eyes. He reminded her of a trapped wolf she'd seen in a television wildlife special—wounded, snarling and lashing out at the humans around him.

"Both of them, actually," Charlie commented. "They're damn fast, those boys. And tough—they'll do to cross the border with."

Just then, one of the men threw a punch and connected with Josh's midriff. The punch caught him unaware and he doubled over before slamming his fist into the man's gut in retribution.

Lucas caught Josh's shoulder in one hand and bent forward to say something to him and once again, Jennifer saw Josh shake his head in refusal. Lucas's shoulders moved in a small shrug of acceptance and he turned toward the door. Jennifer thought he was giving up, but then he turned and with lightning swiftness, clipped Josh's chin with a hard right. Josh crumpled and Lucas caught him before he hit the floor, bending to sling him over his shoulder. Murphy ran interference on their way to the door, the tall blond man covering their backs.

Charlie yanked open the door and pulled Jennifer outside just before the four men reached them. The door swished shut behind them and Lucas strode off down the sidewalk, halting in front of the lighted window of the hardware store next to the saloon.

"Where are you parked, Zach? My truck's all the way back at the fairground."

"Just across the street."

Lucas hitched Josh higher. "We'll put him in the back of your truck, if that's all right."

"Sure," Colby started off across the street.

Jennifer stepped off the curb beside Lucas, walking beside him as he quickly crossed the empty street. Josh's head bumped against Lucas's back with each step his brother took, his body limp where it lay across one broad shoulder.

"Is he all right?" she asked worriedly, glancing at Josh's bobbing head.

"He will be," Lucas said grimly. "He's out cold, but not just because I hit him. I could smell the whiskey on him a mile away."

"Oh."

Colby let down the tailgate on the truck and Lucas rolled the unconscious Josh off his shoulder and onto the metal truck bed. Colby and Murphy vaulted up onto the tailgate and grabbed Josh's arms, pulling him farther into the truck bed so that Lucas could close the tailgate.

"Why don't you drive, Lucas?" Colby tossed him the keys. "I'll ride back here with Murphy and keep Josh from sliding around."

"All right." Lucas caught the keys and took Jennifer's arm. "I'll drop Jennifer off first."

"Sure."

Jennifer climbed into the cab and slid beneath the wheel to the passenger side. Lucas got in beside her and started the truck, backing it out of the parking space and negotiating the short blocks to her little house without saying a word.

He left the truck idling while he walked her to the door, waiting until she unlocked the door and pushed it inward before he spoke.

"I'm sorry tonight ended like this," he told her stiffly. "Sorry you had to see Josh this way."

"Was he like this before Sarah left?" Jennifer asked softly, aching for the pain she read on his face.

"No. He's always been a little wild—hell, so was I," Lucas admitted tiredly. "But not like this. Ever since Sarah left, he's been getting worse, almost as if he's self-destructing. And I can't seem to help him," he added gruffly.

Jennifer smoothed her palm over his cheek and stroked his bottom lip with the pad of her thumb. "You can't protect him all the time, Lucas, or keep his world safe. That's what you told me about Trey, remember? And you were right. Josh has a good heart, just like Trey—he'll come through this."

Lucas wrapped his arms around her and hugged her tight. "God, I hope so," he muttered fervently. He pressed a kiss against her soft mouth and released her. "I have to go. I'll call you."

"Good night," Jennifer called after him as he strode down her sidewalk and climbed into the truck. Charlie lifted a hand in farewell as the pickup pulled away from the curb. She watched until it disappeared around the corner at the end of the block before she went into the house and closed the door. Her heart ached for Lucas.

"Josh, you've got to stop this."

Josh glared at Lucas from his one good eye and stalked, limping, across the linoleum floor to the coffeepot.

Lucas eyed him, assessing the damage. His brother's left eye was swollen nearly shut, and his jaw carried a bruise that was turning blue and faintly purple. Lucas hid a grimace behind his coffee mug; he knew that bruise was located exactly where his own fist had connected with Josh's chin the night before.

Jeans were the only clothing Josh had pulled on when he'd rolled out of bed, and his bare torso held a variety of bruises, large and small, where blows had caught him.

He poured a mug of coffee and limped to the table, wincing as he settled into a chair across from Lucas.

"Ed Bates already called this morning with a tally on the damages to the Wild Horse last night."

Josh looked up. "So? How bad is it?"

Lucas gave him a dollar figure and he winced.

"That bad, huh?"

"You and Zach Colby did a hell of a lot of damage before we got there."

"I'll pay the tab. It was my fault, not Zach's," Josh muttered. "I remember him trying to talk me out of it, but, hell, I guess I didn't want to be talked out of anything."

"No, I guess you didn't," Lucas said dryly. "I tried to talk you into leaving the saloon and you refused."

"I vaguely remember." Josh narrowed his one good eye at his brother. "And then the lights went out." He fingered his jaw and the darkening bruise. "Is that when you gave me this?"

"Yeah. You've got to stop drinking and fighting, Josh. It's not going to bring Sarah back."

Josh stiffened in his chair, staring into the thick blackness of his coffee. "What makes you think I'm doing this because of Sarah?"

"Don't tap-dance around this. The woman left town and you went straight to hell in a hand basket!"

Josh rubbed his forehead and slouched lower in the chair. "She didn't even say goodbye," he muttered. He stared out the window, eyes distant. "I could understand her leaving if we'd had a fight, or if I'd done something wrong, but this..." His voice trailed off. The silence in the kitchen was broken only by the ticking of the old clock above the refrigerator. His glance flicked back to Lucas, his face somber. "I feel like the heart's been ripped right out of me, Lucas. There's nothing left inside except a big, empty hole."

Lucas couldn't remember the last time he'd cried, but he was afraid he was going to now. The desolation in Josh's eyes was unbearable.

"She's not worth it," he growled, his voice gravelly. "No woman's worth this, Josh."

His eyes sad, Josh's mouth nevertheless lifted in a brief smile. "Oh, yeah? What if it was you, and this was Jennifer we were talking about?"

Lucas couldn't answer him. The thought of Jennifer leaving was unthinkable; that she would leave without telling him why, beyond bearing.

"You don't have to answer, Lucas," Josh said softly. "I can tell by the look on your face that you'd feel exactly the way I do. Tell me, big brother, are you going to marry that woman?"

Lucas's head jerked up.

"Of course not," he said automatically. "I'm never getting married. Women are more trouble than they're worth."

"Lucas," Josh said, shaking his head in commiseration, "*most* women are more trouble than they're worth, but if a man is lucky enough to come across one who isn't, he'd be a damn fool not to marry her." He pushed himself upright and leaned his palms on the table to look Lucas in the eye. "And you, brother, are no fool."

Lucas didn't answer. He sat there in silence and watched Josh pick up his mug and limp his way out of the kitchen.

He had no answers for Josh's torment, no solution to end his brother's grieving.

Neither did he have an answer to Josh's question about marriage. Murphy had asked him the same question in almost the same words earlier that morning, and he hadn't had an answer then, either. Frustrated, he tossed the rest of his coffee down the sink, rinsed out his mug and headed for the barn.

"What a beautiful day!" Jennifer dropped her head back, inhaled deeply and threw her arms wide. The sun warmed her upturned face and bare arms, the late-morning breeze lifting the loose ends of her braid and teasing her nostrils with the smell of sage.

Lucas untied the blanket from behind his saddle and grinned at her. "You got lucky, city girl," he teased. "It rained this morning, just enough to settle the dust and cool the air. Otherwise, we'd be sweating bullets by now.''

"Glowing," she corrected him, walking closer to catch the far side of the blanket. "Ladies glow, men sweat.''

He chuckled, a deep rich sound that brought a smile to her face. "Let me guess, you got that from Annabel, right?''

"Actually, yes."

They spread the blanket on the rough ground and Lucas retrieved a saddlebag of food before he joined Jennifer on the square. She sat cross-legged, using binoculars to slowly search the horizon.

"I can see forever," she murmured. She lowered the binoculars and looked at him. "This is probably old hat to you, Lucas, but I love climbing this butte." She twisted to look behind her at the haphazard tower of flat stones. "And seeing the stones the shepherds left." She leaned over and dropped an impulsive kiss on his lean cheek. "Thank you for bringing me."

Lucas shrugged. "I had to ride up here anyway to check on the spring and make sure that bull of Hildebrand's hadn't broken through the fence again.''

"Well, I'm glad you brought me along." Jennifer turned back to the sweeping, three-hundred-and-sixty-degree view spread out below them. "Montana is such a beautiful place, don't you think?''

"Mmm," Lucas replied. "I've always thought so, but a lot of people hate the lack of trees."

"Not me. I like trees, but this is . . . indescribable. There's just something about all this open space that makes me feel so free."

"It strikes me as strange that a woman who was raised in Seattle, surrounded by trees, doesn't miss the evergreens," Lucas reflected, watching her dreamy expression.

"I don't. Perhaps because I lived in the city, not the country. Seattle has more high-rise concrete buildings than pine trees. Or perhaps because my life was always changing, I'm more open to different types of places," she said thoughtfully.

"Always changing? I thought you spent all your life in Seattle."

"I did." She glanced sideways at him. "I didn't mean my place of residence, I meant my home life. I had two stepfathers—sometimes it felt like my mother's emotional life had a revolving door with a big sign on it that said Temporary Help Only."

"Must have been rough." Lucas's quiet voice held sympathy.

"Just when I got used to a new one, he'd leave."

Lucas knew all about parents leaving—first his mother, then his father. "But your mother stayed, right?"

"Oh, yes." Jennifer pulled up a stem of grass and began to shred it, lengthwise, with slow, methodical motions. "She stayed. My sisters and I would console her and hug her when she cried. Each time, I hoped she wouldn't find another man, but then she'd come home one night all starry-eyed and I'd know she'd fallen in love again."

"And that was bad, huh?"

"For my mother, in the end, it was always bad."

"Is she married now?"

"No, she stopped marrying them after number three. Numbers four and five just moved in and lived with her."

"So we both lost our parents early," Lucas mused aloud. "Mine moved on or died, and your mother deserted you emotionally."

Jennifer stopped shredding the blade of grass and looked at him. "That's true," she said slowly.

"Yet another thing we have in common," he said softly.

She smiled briefly, a small, sad smile. "Do we have any good things in common?"

"Sure. You have sisters, I have a brother."

He reached up and curved his palm around the back of her neck, tugging gently until she toppled sideways into his arms. He rolled over and trapped her between his braced forearms, then lowered his head and kissed her. Warm and slow, his mouth cherished hers. He brushed several more kisses across her lips before he lifted his head and looked down at her. "Murphy asked me if we were courting."

"Courting?" Jennifer's half-closed eyes opened and she stared up at him. "What did you tell him?"

"I told him I'm not sure." He brushed a wisp of hair away from her cheek, his fingers lingering against her skin. "What do you think? Are we?"

"I don't know. What does it mean exactly, courting?"

"I think it means that we have honorable intentions," he said gravely, his eyes serious.

"Do we?" she whispered.

He didn't answer her directly. "You're the first woman I've ever met who can defy me one minute and make me laugh the next. You drive me crazy with wanting you until I'm so hot I'm ready to explode, and then you're so damn vulnerable I voluntarily back off. I haven't willingly let a woman into my life for years and one look from those pretty, golden eyes and I found myself agreeing to let you spend your evenings in my living room." He threaded his fingers through the end of her braid and pulled it over her shoulder, smoothing it down over her breast. "So you tell me," he said huskily. "Do I have honorable intentions? Do you?"

"Oh, Lucas." Tears misted her vision, and her voice shook with the force of her emotions. "I—"

Staked a short ten feet away, Lucas's gelding reared suddenly, whinnying loudly and snorting as he sniffed the breeze.

Lucas's head lifted quickly and he glared at the horse.

"What the hell? Satan, what's wrong with you?"

He pushed up to his knees, his gaze scanning the pasture below the butte. Both horses were snorting, stamping their feet and tugging on the staked ropes that held them. Lucas turned his face into the slight wind and inhaled deeply.

"Smoke," he said softly, and reached for Jennifer's discarded binoculars before he stood.

"Lucas? What is it?" Alarmed, Jennifer scrambled to her feet.

"Fire," he said succinctly. He handed her the binoculars and turned to the horses.

Jennifer trained the binoculars on the area north of the butte where Lucas had been searching and found a column of smoke. Just beyond, a tiny human figure jumped down from a piece of farm equipment and ran back toward the red flames that licked at the dry grass.

"Lucas, there's someone down there." She turned to find him rapidly tying the rolled blanket to the back of the saddle, the saddlebags already buckled securely in place.

"I'm pretty sure that's Trey—I sent him up to the north ranch to drive a swathing machine home this afternoon."

"Oh, no." Jennifer's heart lodged in her throat.

"Hurry up," Lucas commanded. He didn't wait for her to mount; instead, he lifted her and tossed her into the saddle, then leaped aboard his own horse.

"Don't try to keep up with me," he ordered. "Ride straight back to the ranch and get Murphy and Charlie—tell them about the fire, they'll know what to do."

"All right. Be careful!" she called after him. But he was already gone. She turned her own mount toward the Lazy H headquarters. "Come on, boy," she murmured to the horse. "I can't ride like Lucas, but I promise you an extra pail of oats if you get me home fast and safe."

She urged the horse forward. Fortunately, the return to the ranch was swift and uneventful and Murphy met her at the barn.

"What's wrong? Where's Lucas?" He caught her horse's bridle strap and reached up a hand to help her down.

"Fire. There's a fire, Murphy!"

"Where?"

"North of the butte. Lucas said he's sure Trey's there—he said something about Trey's driving a swathing machine home this afternoon."

"Yeah, that's where he is." Murphy's words were clipped and incisive. "Charlie's in the bunkhouse—go roust him out and tell him what happened. I'll get the truck while he calls the neighbors."

Charlie phoned the neighbors and hurried out to join her just as Murphy braked to a dust-raising stop next to them and shoved open the door.

"Get in," he barked.

Jennifer scrambled into the truck and slid across the seat to allow room for Charlie. Murphy already had the truck moving before the latch clicked shut.

"Where's Trey?" Charlie asked.

"Lucas thinks he's drivin' the swather home just about where the fire is," Murphy said.

"We saw him from the top of the butte," Jennifer told him.

"Damn fool kid," Charlie muttered. "He should have gone for help."

"He's not alone," Jennifer told him. "He has Lucas with him."

"Plus us," Murphy said firmly. "I can see the smoke—hang on." He left the graveled road and plunged the truck into the shallow ditch.

Jennifer grabbed the dashboard to brace herself as Murphy sent the pickup racing over the rough pasture. The closer they got to the fire, the worse it looked. Murphy slammed to a halt next to the swather and they piled out of the pickup; two figures came running toward them through the smoke.

"It's not as bad as it looks!" Lucas yelled. He had a red bandanna tied over his nose and the lower half of his face and his forehead was streaked with black. His torso was bare, smeared with sweat and soot, and the singed remains of his shirt dangled limply from one hand. "We should be able to contain it with enough help. Did somebody call the neighbors?"

"They're on their way," Charlie yelled back. He climbed into the back of the pickup and slid shovels onto the tailgate.

"Great. Trey, grab one of those shovels, and get back to the south side." He turned to look for Murphy and spotted Jennifer standing by the open cab door, a pile of blankets clutched in her arms. "What the hell are you doing here?" he demanded furiously.

"I came to help put out a fire." She shot him a challenging look. "And don't tell me to go home and wait."

"Stubborn, impossible woman," he muttered impatiently. "Give me one of those blankets."

"Here." Jennifer slapped a blanket into his hand.

He stabbed a finger at her. "You stay away from the fire."

Her only answer was a sniff before she turned her back on him. Fuming, Lucas went back to the fire. It wasn't until nearly an hour later that he looked up and realized that the fire fighter wielding a shovel next to him had a long red-gold braid hanging down her back.

He grabbed the braid and tugged.

Jennifer felt the pull on her hair and spun around, relief flooding her when she realized that it was Lucas.

"Good grief, Lucas, you scared me."

"I ought to do more than scare you," he growled. "I thought I told you to stay out of this smoke."

"I wanted to help," she said stubbornly.

He glared at her, but she didn't back down and Lucas didn't have time to argue with her. "Then stay with me. If you won't go where I know it's safe, at least you'll be close enough for me to make sure you're not in danger."

Jennifer nodded and returned to digging along a section of turned earth that the fire fighters hoped would provide a southern firebreak and stop the slow-moving flames.

Two hours later, their hopes were realized. Lucas stood among the group of neighboring ranchers and surveyed the blackened, fire-singed earth.

"Looks like you lost less than three hundred acres, Lucas," Charlie said, his gaze assessing the damage. "Not bad."

"We're lucky there wasn't much wind," Wes Hildebrand declared. "Back in '62, I saw a prairie fire with a strong wind behind it race over a thousand acres in nothing flat."

The group of weary men nodded in solemn acknowledgment.

"Well, I don't know about you-all, but I'm headin' home for a bath and a shot of whiskey," the white-haired rancher declared.

"That sounds like the best idea I've heard all day, Wes," Murphy agreed. "What do you say, boss, you ready?"

Lucas's gaze left the blackened acres, where he'd been searching, without results, for any overlooked patches of smoldering grass, and flicked over Jennifer's tired face before he nodded at Murphy.

"I'm ready, let's go home."

Jennifer trudged to the parked truck and climbed wearily into the cab. She left the door open to encourage the breeze, but the interior of the cab was still stiflingly hot.

Charlie, Murphy and Trey climbed into the bed of the pickup. Lucas pulled open the driver's-side door and slid behind the wheel.

"It looks awful," she commented, gazing out at the blackened acres of pasture as she pulled the door shut.

"It could have been a lot worse," Lucas replied, concentrating on easing the truck over the uneven pasture ground. "It could have burnt more acres, we could have lost livestock or someone could have been hurt worse than they were."

She twisted around to face him. "Someone was hurt? Who? How?"

"Wes twisted an ankle when he stepped in a hole, that's all. The rest of us picked up a few burns, but all minor."

Jennifer searched quickly over him. He was so covered with soot, sweat and dirt that she couldn't tell if he was hurt. "Did you get burned?"

"A little." He caught her worried frown. "It's nothing."

"I'll be the judge of that," she said fiercely. "Where? Show me."

He lifted his left hand away from the steering wheel and turned it over.

Jennifer sucked in her breath. His palm had broken blisters, and the inside of his forearm held angry red burn marks.

"Lucas Hightower, that's not minor!"

"Sure it is." He returned his hand to the steering wheel. "Don't get all excited. I'll put some salve on it when we get home."

"I'll look at it after you've showered," Jennifer said firmly. "Then we'll either go to the hospital emergency room or I'll bandage it myself."

Lucas grinned at her. "Yes, ma'am. You sure are a bossy little thing."

"This isn't funny, Lucas, don't argue with me," she ordered.

"Oh, no," he said solemnly, hiding a grin. "I'd never do that."

Lucas eased the truck in and out of the ditch and onto the level surface of graveled road.

Jennifer breathed a sigh of relief and tilted her face to the wind that whipped in through the window when he accelerated. She looked back at the burnt pasture, quickly disappearing from view as they sped down the road, and watched the neighbors' pickups following the same route.

Suddenly, Jennifer realized that she hadn't seen Josh all day. "Where is Josh?"

"He and Zach Colby went to Glasgow to look at a registered quarter horse mare Zach's thinking about buying." Lucas braked to a stop in front of the house and flashed a tired grin. "He'll be sorry he missed all the fun."

"Fun?" Jennifer gave him a withering look. "You have the most bizarre notion of fun of anyone I've ever met."

Lucas chuckled and stepped out of the cab. Murphy, Charlie and Trey were climbing stiffly out of the back. Jennifer shoved open her door and hurried to intercept them.

"We'll take turns in the shower and crash for a while," Murphy said to Lucas. "Don't worry if none of us show up for dinner—we'll make sandwiches or something when we wake up."

"Which isn't likely to be anytime soon," Charlie said, flexing a sore arm. "I feel like I've been rode hard and put away wet. How about you, kid?"

Trey managed a tired grin, but he was swaying on his feet with exhaustion.

"Wait a minute—before you leave, tell me if anyone got burned," Jennifer demanded.

"Nope—just minor stuff," Murphy reassured her.

"That's what Lucas said." She threw him a dark glance. "Show me."

One by one, Murphy, Charlie and Trey stood in front of her. She inspected small burns and scrapes on hands and arms and a slight cut near Charlie's eye, but nothing that soap, water and burn salve wouldn't cure.

"All right, I guess you'll all survive."

"What about you?" Murphy asked, casting a critical eye over her soot-smudged jeans and shirt.

"I didn't get a scratch," she said with a smile.

"Good." Murphy nodded in satisfaction. "Well, I'm gonna go try to wash this smoke off me." Murphy turned and headed for the bunkhouse.

Trey gave her a weary smile and followed him and Charlie.

"Are you satisfied that all your boys are safe?" Lucas said softly.

"Yes," she said, sweeping a critical glance over his dirty frame. "Except for you. But you're going to have to scrub that black stuff off before I can tell just how damaged you are."

"Not a bad idea." Lucas took her arm and steered her toward the house. "But you get first turn in the shower."

Jennifer argued with him, but to no avail. He insisted that she shower before him. Her outer clothing was filthy, and even her bra, panties and socks were permeated with the smell of smoke. She stripped them off and dropped them in a pile on the floor.

The old-fashioned bathroom had a shower stall in addition to a tub; Jennifer soaped her hair three times before she could no longer smell smoke. Mindful that she shouldn't empty the hot-water tank, she scrubbed her skin quickly, turned off the water and opened the shower door.

Steam billowed out the door and she stepped onto the mat, grabbed a towel and quickly closed the door. She had rubbed herself dry, wiped the steam from the mirror and run a comb through the tangles in her hair before she realized that her clothes were gone.

Chapter Eleven

Jennifer wrapped the big towel around her and opened the door, poking her head out to look up and down the empty hallway.

"Lucas!"

"Yeah?"

Wearing only clean faded jeans, he appeared in the doorway of a bedroom on the other side of the hall.

"Where are my clothes?"

"I put them in the washer with mine. Why?"

"First of all, I don't have anything else to wear," she began.

"You can borrow one of my shirts," he interjected. "What's second?"

"Second, just how did you get my clothes?"

"I walked into the bathroom and took them. You didn't hear me? The shower was running—the sound of the water must have kept you from hearing me."

Jennifer eyed his innocent expression and tried to remember just how opaque the shower door was. ''Where's the shirt?''

''Right here.'' Lucas disappeared and quickly reappeared, a long-sleeved white cotton shirt in his hand.

Jennifer stretched out an arm around the edge of the door and took the shirt from him. ''Turn around.''

He obeyed and she slipped out of the bathroom and across the hall into the bedroom he'd just vacated. ''All right,'' she called through the closed door. ''You can turn around now.''

She thought she heard him chuckle before the bathroom door closed. Moments later, the sound of running water told her that he was in the shower. Hurriedly, she dropped the towel and shoved her arms into the sleeves of the shirt. It was huge on her; the shoulder seams reached halfway to her elbows, and the long tails reached almost to her knees with the curved-up hemmed sides exposing bare skin from knee to midthigh. She fumbled with the pearl snaps that closed the front, but the cuffs kept falling down over her hands, making it impossible to see. Impatiently, she rolled the sleeves up to her elbows and quickly snapped the shirt closed.

She snatched her wet towel and opened the bedroom door. The shower was still running and she sighed with relief; she was determined to catch Lucas and examine the burns on his arm and hand as soon as he got back into his jeans. Blotting the water from her hair with a towel, she crossed the hallway and leaned against the wall next to the bathroom door.

Short minutes later, the shower shut off. Jennifer counted to fifty before she knocked on the door.

"Lucas, are you decent? If you're dressed, let me in."

There was no answer.

"Lucas? Let me in—I want to see your hand."

The door opened and he eyed her. "It doesn't take a genius to spread some salve on my hand. I can manage it."

"I'm sure you can," she said determinedly, stepping forward and planting her palm flat on his bare chest. She nudged him backward and he gave way until the backs of his knees touched the commode. "Sit."

He glared at her, but he sat.

"Let me see your arm...please," she added when he only stared at her.

He held out his arm, palm up, and Jennifer gasped softly.

"Oh, Lucas." She gently took his big hand in hers, stepping closer to inspect the raw, broken blisters on his palm she'd noted earlier and the three uneven stripes of angry red burns on the inside of his forearm. "How did this happen?"

"Trey's shirt caught fire. I ripped it off his back and rolled him on the ground. To tell you the truth, I didn't even know I'd burned myself until about an hour later."

"But Trey wasn't burned?"

"No, I must have grabbed him at almost the same time his shirt started burning. The poor kid was so upset about starting the fire, he probably wouldn't have realized he was on fire himself until he'd burned to a cinder."

Jennifer looked up in surprise. "Trey started the fire?"

"Actually, a spark from the swather he was driving started it. He didn't even know the grass was burning until he was almost a quarter of a mile away, when he looked behind him and saw it."

"Hmm." She shook her head. "We're lucky no one got hurt badly." She laid his hand, palm up, on his thigh and picked up a tube of salve from the counter-top. "I don't think we need to take you to the emergency room, but you need salve on those burns and bandages on the blisters."

She picked up his hand and stepped between his spread legs while she concentrated on gently rubbing the salve over the torn skin of his palm.

Jennifer seemed oblivious to the intimacy of the small, steamy, heated bathroom, but Lucas was vividly aware that she couldn't be wearing anything but her smooth, soft skin under his white shirt.

He knew because he'd deposited her bra and panties in the washer himself. A bra that was nothing more than a wisp of lavender lace and satin, and panties that were even less substantial. For a moment, he wished fervently that he hadn't tossed her underwear in with the rest of the clothes; it would have been such pleasure to stroke them off her.

"Does this hurt?"

"No," he said, distracted by the shadow where the white shirt collar fell open below her collarbone. The shirt was miles too big and the first closed snap caught the front together just between her breasts.

"There." She screwed the lid back on the tube of salve and stepped away from him to reach a box of gauze. "This should only take a minute and we'll be done."

She stepped back between his legs, turning sideways to rest his elbow on the edge of the sink counter. "Hold your hand up so I can wrap the gauze around your palm."

He complied, but the back of her knee brushed against his other hand where it rested on his inner thigh. He rubbed the back of his fingers against silky skin and nearly groaned with the sensation.

"Lucas." Jennifer glanced down at him to protest just as his hand splayed wide over the back of her thigh just above her knee. Her eyes widened, her pulse beginning a slow, steady throb as she met his heavy-lidded gaze. "I think you're violating the 'nothing below the waist' rule," she whispered.

"Nope," he denied, his own voice lowered to an intimate murmur. "Legs are legal."

She gave him a disbelieving look and he smiled lazily, his fingers moving in slow, arousing circles against her sensitive skin.

"Aren't you going to finish the bandage?" he asked her.

Jennifer turned back to wrapping his palm with the gauze, but his warm hand, moving in small, stroking movements against her leg, was a distraction difficult to ignore. Relieved when the ends of white gauze were securely tied, she turned to face him, her gaze searching his face, neck, shoulders and chest.

"Your hand and arm weren't the only places that were injured," she scolded gently. The smooth skin of his chest was marred by several reddened spots, some as large as a fifty-cent piece, some as small as a dime. "You didn't tell me about these."

"I didn't even know I had them until I showered."

"That's understandable." She turned away to pick up the tube of salve. "You were smeared with soot."

She squeezed the salve onto her fingertips and bent closer to smooth it over his reddened skin. His muscles jerked, tensing under her fingers, and she snatched her hand away, glancing up at him with quick concern. "Does that hurt?"

"No," Lucas said through his teeth. "It doesn't hurt—it feels good. Don't stop."

Carefully, she went back to rubbing the cool salve over the burns, glancing up frequently into his face to gauge his reaction. "Are you sure I'm not hurting you?" she asked as she spread the gel over the last tiny red mark on his abdomen just above his navel. The washboard muscles under her fingers jumped in reaction at each soothing stroke, his hand on her thigh tensing and easing with each twitch of muscle.

"You're killing me," he muttered in a throaty rasp.

Startled, she looked into his face. His eyes gleamed with blue heat from between lowered black lashes. She'd tried to ignore her own sensual awareness that grew with each stroke of her fingers over his sleek, hot skin, but it burned higher, hotter, weakening her resolve.

"Lucas," she said slowly. "I don't think—"

"Don't think," he ordered softly. "Put down the salve."

"But I'm not sure I covered all the places you were hurt," she objected. "Let me check your back."

"That's not where I hurt," he said, "and that's not where I'm burning. Put down the salve."

She stared at him without speaking, tube in one hand, its cap in the other. Jennifer knew what he was telling her. He wanted to make love to her, and he wanted her willing; still, she knew he'd let her go if she refused him.

"I'm not protected," she whispered at last, her eyes solemn.

"I'll take care of you." His voice was a husky whisper.

Jennifer stared into his eyes. He could have easily seduced her into submission, but instead, he sat waiting, his body tense with self-imposed restraint.

Without taking her gaze from his, she carefully replaced the cap with trembling hands and reached behind her to drop the tube into the sink. Then she reached out and curved her hands over his shoulders.

His eyes narrowed; his breath rushed out in an audible hiss. His bandaged hand caught the front of her shirt and with a twist, popped the top two snaps open. Jennifer gasped and his fingers tightened on the back of her thigh, urging her a step forward at the same time that he buried his face against the soft, fragrant valley between her breasts.

Thick black hair brushed silkily against her skin when he turned his head, and her hands left his shoulders to cradle him against her, his mouth moving in hot, tasting kisses over the inner curve of her breast.

"Lucas," she breathed. "Please..."

He heard her. His cheek brushed against her nipple before his mouth found her, and the hot, wet suction buckled her knees. She sagged against him and he ripped open the remaining snaps on her shirt, his hand moving higher on her thigh as he urged her forward. She stumbled and he slid his legs between hers and drew her down to sit on his thighs, palming the curve of her bottom to pull her closer.

His mouth left her breast and he lifted his head to look at her, his throat going dry. The white shirt hung open down the front, nearly falling off one slender shoulder. The still-damp, wildly curling thickness of her hair tumbled around her shoulders in a vivid, glorious mane. His gaze followed the path of his fingers as they brushed slowly from her collarbone, down over the rose-tipped creamy swell of one breast and the inward curve of her waist to the flare of hips and the thatch of red-gold curls between. He brushed the backs of his fingers against the silky curls, and looked back up at her.

"I don't want to hurt you," he managed to whisper roughly. "You're bound to be small and I'm not sure I can be gentle. It's been too long and I want you too much."

"You won't hurt me." Jennifer's voice was slurred. "I want you, too." She smoothed her fingers over his lips and leaned forward, her mouth covering his. The tips of her breasts brushed against his chest and she crowded closer, instinctively seeking contact with the heat that radiated from his body.

Lucas groaned. He caught the back of her head in one big palm and crushed her mouth under his, while his other hand cupped her bottom and pulled her hips tight against his.

Pleasure exploded. Jennifer slid her fingers into his hair and pressed him closer while she fed off the hot, exciting flavors of his mouth. His tongue surged and withdrew and her hips instinctively sought his in answering movements. She was naked against the hard ridge of his jeans, but the interfering denim quickly became unbearable and her hands left his hair to tug at the metal buttons that kept her from him.

Lucas tore his mouth away from hers and groaned. "Damn, honey, don't do that!" He pressed her hands hard against him, his eyes squeezing shut in pleasure and torment.

He opened them to see Jennifer's flushed, passion-drowsy features looking at him with confusion.

"We can't do this here," he said, sliding his arms under her and standing up.

"Why not?"

"Because your protection is in my bedroom." He leaned over to open the bathroom door and she clutched him, her arms slipping around his neck to hold on, her legs wrapped around his waist. She nibbled on his throat; he groaned, crossed the hall in two strides and kicked his bedroom door shut behind him, flipping the lock.

The shades were drawn against the afternoon heat, the room cool and shadowy when Lucas set her on her feet beside the bed.

He laid his palms flat on the soft, bare skin of her shoulders inside her shirt.

"Let's get rid of this," he whispered. She nodded and he slipped the white cotton from her shoulders. It fell to the floor, pooling around her feet. His gaze brushed over her nude body, lingering on the upward tilt of full, pink-tipped breasts, the inward curve of small waist, the outward flare of hips and long length of leg that ended in small, pink-tipped toes. "You're beautiful," he said, his voice hushed, thick and harsh with emotion. "The most beautiful woman I've ever seen."

She swayed and reached for him, her hands closing over his waist, and he wrapped her close, his mouth taking hers with hot insistence as he tumbled with her, twisting so that he landed beneath her on the bed. His hands stroked over her back and closed over the curve of her bottom, pressing her hard against him. She squirmed and he groaned, rolling with her so that she lay beneath him, the bed sheets cool against her back. Her hands were busy, traveling over the hot skin of his shoulders and back, pulling him closer when he moved to lift himself away.

"Let me up, honey, I have to get my jeans off." He kissed her hard and pushed up.

Jennifer lay sprawled on the bed, watching him through half-closed eyes as he stripped off his jeans and took something out of a drawer in the bedside table.

Lucas turned and saw her watching him, her hot stare sending his pulse shuddering.

"I can't wait any longer," he said thickly, dropping back beside her on the bed. She curled toward him, her mouth finding his, and he barely managed to sheath himself before he pushed her onto her back and covered her, wedging a place for himself between her thighs.

Jennifer tensed, her fingers curling tightly over his biceps. She trusted Lucas, but her memory of what was about to happen wasn't pleasant. He braced his forearms and looked down at her, smoothing clinging tendrils of damp hair away from her face.

"Relax, honey, let me in," he whispered. He flexed his hips, pushing with controlled, insistent nudges against her soft heat. "If it hurts, tell me, and I'll stop."

Her gaze clung to his as he continued to croon to her, soothing murmurs underlined with the reassuring, continuous strokes of his fingers against her cheeks, throat and breasts. A fine sheen of sweat broke out on his forehead, his fingers trembling as he linked them ever closer. Jennifer's apprehension fled, replaced by a new kind of tension as she adjusted to the heavy, intrusive heat of his body with tiny, shivering movements of inner muscles.

Lucas saw passion replace the apprehension on her flushed features, felt the subtle lift of her hips against his and surged forward with a groan.

He tried to remember to be gentle. Jennifer wouldn't let him. Still, he held off his own completion until she was sobbing beneath him, pleading for release, before he tumbled them both off the edge and into oblivion.

Jennifer lay pinned beneath Lucas; his breath was harsh in her ear and his heavy weight should have crushed her, but she welcomed the warm dampness of skin against skin. She stared up at the ceiling.

Lucas lifted himself onto one elbow and shifted his weight off of her. She was smiling, a slow, satisfied curving of her mouth that was entrancing, and when her gaze left the ceiling and moved to him, her eyes were glowing.

"My goodness," she breathed in awe. "Why didn't you tell me what I'd been missing?"

Lucas grinned and ran a forefinger down the length of her nose. "I told you we should throw out the above-the-waist rule, but you wouldn't listen."

"You're amazing." She eyed him with fascination. "Is it always like that?"

Lucas's grin faded, his features intent and serious. "Honey, it's never been like that before."

"Fireworks?" she asked softly. "And skyrockets?"

"All of those," he agreed. "With maybe an atom bomb or two thrown in."

"Do you suppose it will always be like that—with us?"

"I damn sure hope so." He moved a hand down her throat and cupped her breast, his thumb circling the pink crest with small, arousing movements.

"So do I." Jennifer half closed her eyes and pushed against his hand. "Maybe we should try again—to find out if it will be the same."

Lucas's hand stilled. He pressed a hard kiss against her mouth and rolled away from her.

"Where are you going?" She pushed up onto one elbow, her hair falling in a silky tumble over her shoulder to cover one bare breast. His back to her, she couldn't see what he was doing until he opened the nightstand drawer. The size of the box of condoms that he set on top of the stand had her eyes widening in shock.

He glanced over his shoulder and paused when he saw the suspicion written on her face. "What's the matter?"

"How long have you kept a giant economy-size box of condoms in your bedroom drawer?"

Lucas laughed, ripped open one of the packets and lay down beside her. "Ever since I decided that sooner or later we were going to end up here. It was inevitable—and I knew damn well that having one or two of them wasn't going to be nearly enough."

"Oh." Barely an inch separated their lips. "In that case, since you have so many of them and all, can I try putting on the next one?"

Lucas's eyes gleamed hotter. "Sure, honey," he murmured. "We'll keep trying until you get it right."

It took several tries, all ending with heavy breathing and earthshaking results. Exhausted, Jennifer fell asleep in Lucas's arms while outside the bedroom window, the sun sank below the horizon and day faded into dusk.

The shrill ringing of the telephone wakened Lucas; he swore, knocking the box of condoms onto the floor as he fumbled on the nightstand to pick up the receiver.

"Yeah?"

"Lucas?"

"Yeah, Josh, it's me. What do you want?"

"You sound like I woke you up—were you sleeping?"

"Yes, dammit, I was sleeping," Lucas snarled with irritation. "What do you want?"

"Are you sick?"

"No, I'm not sick."

"Then why are you asleep at eight-thirty at night?"

"Everybody's asleep," Lucas said, stretching the truth. He really didn't know if Charlie, Murphy and Trey were awake or not. "We had a fire in the pasture north of the butte and after we put it out, we all came home, took showers and collapsed."

"Damn," Josh swore succinctly. "Did anybody get hurt?"

"No, we're all fine."

"How many acres did it burn?"

"Less than three hundred." Lucas felt Jennifer slip her arms around his waist, her soft breasts snuggled against his back. "Did you call for a reason?"

"Oh, yeah. I need you to come take a look at a mare of Zach's. Do you feel up to it?"

Lucas frowned. "What's wrong with her?"

"She's trying to foal, but she's been in labor too long. Zach called the vet, but he's on the other side of the county and isn't expected back for hours."

"Damn," Lucas swore in frustration. "All right, give me a half hour. I'll be there."

"Thanks, Lucas."

Lucas dropped the receiver into its cradle and rolled onto his back, pulling Jennifer on top of him and locking her against him in the circle of his arms.

"I have to go over to Colby's," he told her. His palms smoothed over the curve of her bottom and pressed her closer. "He has a mare that's having trouble dropping a foal."

"Oh." Jennifer's gaze flicked to the darkened window before returning to his face. "It's late. I need to go home and feed Beastie."

"I wish you didn't have to leave," he said huskily. "I like the idea of finding you waiting in my bed when I get back."

She smiled and shook her head. "I can't."

He caught the back of her head in one palm, rolled over and crushed her mouth under his. When he let her go and sat up on the edge of the bed, she was breathless. She tugged the sheet over her and watched in silence as he stood and pulled on his jeans, shrugged into a shirt and took a pair of socks out of the bureau drawer.

He sat back down on the edge of the bed to pull on socks and boots, standing to stamp his feet into them, then leaned over to pick up the box of condoms from the floor and return it to the drawer.

"Sure you won't change your mind and stay?"

"No, I can't." She shook her head.

He leaned one knee on the mattress and bent over the bed to press a last, swift kiss against her mouth.

"I have to go," he said reluctantly. "Be careful driving home."

"I will."

He paused at the door, his gaze sweeping her length with one last, searing glance. Then he yanked open the door and stepped through, pulling it shut behind him.

Jennifer lay without moving, staring at the ceiling for long moments before she tossed back the sheet and got out of bed.

Her clothes were still wet in the washing machine. Jennifer raided Lucas's closet for a T-shirt and a pair of jeans; the jeans were so long she had to roll them more than once and only the cinched-in leather belt she found kept them from falling off her hips.

No lights shone from the bunkhouse windows; nevertheless, Jennifer heaved a sigh of relief when she collected her wet clothes, started her car and left the Lazy H without being intercepted.

Beastie greeted her at her door with tail-wagging delight, luxuriating in the affectionate pats and satisfying scratches she gave him behind his ears. He followed her into the kitchen and flopped down on the rug in front of the stove, panting happily while she measured dog food into his bowl.

She set the bowl down on the floor and the big Lab jumped to his feet and lowered his head to eat. Jennifer leaned against the counter and slowly slid to the floor, her back against the wooden cabinet door, her chin resting on her knees drawn up to her chest. She hugged her knees close and watched the dog.

"Beastie," she said with stark honesty, "I've done a very foolish thing. I've fallen in love with Lucas Hightower."

Beastie lifted his head, cocked his ears at her and gave a soft woof of sympathy before lowering his muzzle back into his dish.

"I'm not sure he'll ever love me back. In fact," she added dismally, "I'm not sure he can, given what happened with his parents. He never said that he loved me—only that he wanted me. And he was right about that," she told the dog. "Making love with Lucas was better than anything I ever imagined—I never knew it was possible to feel so much pleasure."

She stared at the dog, her eyes brooding and dark. "I'm not sure I can handle an affair—not after watching my mother suffer through so much insecurity and heartache."

Ruling out an affair left only two options; celibacy or marriage. Marriage terrified her almost as much as the thought of an affair, and the possibility of never making love to Lucas again sent a sharp, stabbing pain through her heart.

"I could leave," she told Beastie. He'd finished emptying his bowl and was busy licking the inside for any traces of food, nudging it across the linoleum with each swipe of his tongue. "I could run away, as far and as fast as possible, and never see him again. Maybe, in time, I'd get over him."

The thought of never seeing his face again, never hearing him laugh, or growl at her to put her hat on in the sun, only increased the ache in her chest.

"I don't know what to do, Beastie," she whispered mournfully. He left his pursuit of his food bowl and returned to her side, flopping down with his head resting on her feet. "I'm scared that I'm just like my mother. I want Lucas so badly that I'm afraid I'll lose me if I let myself love him. Would loving Lucas destroy me or am I strong enough to make this love last a lifetime?"

Beastie lifted his head and stared at her with brown, soulful eyes.

"Maybe if he loves me, too," she whispered into his sympathetic face, "we can make it work. Maybe I don't have to be strong enough on my own, maybe it takes two people equally in love to make it last forever."

Beastie's pink tongue lapped at her hand in silent comfort. Jennifer accepted his unconditional affection, hugging him fiercely before she stood up.

"Let's go to bed, Beastie. Tomorrow we have to go out to the Lazy H, and I have to talk to Lucas."

Jennifer tossed and turned most of the night, falling asleep just when the sun lifted its head over the horizon. As a consequence, she slept late, and the morning was nearly gone before she reached the Lazy H.

Her knock on the screen door got no response at the house, but Lucas's pickup was parked in front of the barn. She set off across the yard lot, her steps slowing as she reached the big doors and heard raised voices.

"And I'm telling you it's none of your business," Josh snarled. "I'll do whatever the hell I want to with my life."

"I'm not going to stand by and watch you kill yourself!" Lucas roared. "You've got to stop grieving over that damn woman and get on with living."

Josh swore at him. "Stop calling her that damn woman—she's got a name."

Jennifer stepped through the doorway in time to see Josh swing at Lucas. She gasped, but Lucas ducked the blow and caught Josh on the chin with a right cross that sent him staggering.

"I don't want to fight you, Josh," Lucas said wearily, regret staining his tones.

"Yeah, right," Josh snarled. "Nagging a man about a woman is getting to be a habit with you. Were you haranguing Clay about a woman before the fight that killed him? Is that why he fought you?"

Jennifer saw the words hit Lucas like a blow, saw him flinch and pale beneath his tan.

"Aw, hell, Lucas." Josh shook his head, sagging against a pole. "I'm sorry, that was a low blow. I shouldn't have said that—you know I didn't mean it."

Lucas didn't answer him. He turned away and went perfectly still, his gaze fastened on Trey's white face. The teenager stood in the doorway to the tack room, a polishing cloth hanging forgotten from one hand.

"Is that true, what Josh said?" His voice shook. "Did you fight with my dad? Did you kill him?"

"We had a fight the night he died." Lucas's voice was flat, no expression, no emotion at all in the grim tones.

"You son of a bitch." Trey's eyes filled, his hands closing into fists. "That's why my mother hates you, isn't it?"

"Yeah," Lucas agreed bleakly. "That's why she hates me."

Trey glared at him, bitter disillusionment and anger carving lines on his young face. "I wish it had been you. It should have been you that died, not my dad."

His voice, like Lucas's, was expressionless, and he turned and walked out of the barn.

He strode past Jennifer without seeming to see her, and Lucas stood motionless, staring at the empty doorway where the teenager had disappeared.

"Lucas," she said softly, wincing when he looked at her. His eyes held old, bone-deep pain, and resignation etched brackets beside his mouth.

"I'm sorry, Lucas." Josh's gaze met his brother's with apology. "I'm so damn sorry. It's not true, not a word of it. I'll go find the boy and explain."

"There's nothing to explain." Lucas sighed and scrubbed a hand down his face. "What you said is true—Clay and I argued over a woman, and we fought. And he died."

"That's not the whole story," Josh argued. "That's not even close to all of it. Clay's death was an accident. If anyone was to blame, it was Suzie, not you."

"Blaming Suzie doesn't make me any less guilty," Lucas said rawly.

"Aw, hell, Lucas," Josh objected. "You can't—"

The sound of hoofbeats interrupted his words and Jennifer looked out the open door just as Trey rode out of the corral on Satan.

"Lucas," she cried, "you have to go after him!"

"I don't know what to say to him," he said, his face dark and brooding as he stared after the boy.

"Tell him the truth." Jennifer slid her arms around his waist and looked up into his face. "He's spent the summer learning to know and respect you—he'll listen. And even if the truth is painful, hearing it is the only chance either of you have to deal with this."

Unconvinced, Lucas looked down into her face.

"Maybe hearing the truth will only make it harder for him to accept his mother, and me."

"I think you're selling Trey short, Lucas. He's stronger than that."

"She's right, Lucas." Josh's deep voice held quiet conviction. "You're both stronger than you think you are."

Lucas glanced from Jennifer's worried face to his brother's. They were the two people he loved most in the world, and who loved him back.

He decided to listen to them.

Lucas made short work of saddling Josh's mare. Josh opened the corral gate and Lucas paused, catching Jennifer's chin in one hand and pressing a warm, hard kiss against her lips.

"When I get back, we need to talk," he murmured, holding her gaze with his.

"Yes," she agreed gravely. "We do—we will."

He smiled briefly, kissed her again and shoved his foot into the stirrup. The mare was moving before he swung his leg over her back, and Lucas settled easily into the saddle. He touched the brim of his hat as he passed Josh, lifting the mare into a ground-eating lope as soon as they cleared the corral.

Lucas knew Trey was watching him long before he sent the mare lunging up the last steep slope of the butte. He was encouraged by the fact that the teenager didn't ride away, but the grim features and shuttered eyes that met his when he dropped onto the ground beside him didn't raise his hopes.

"I guess we need to talk," he said bluntly.

"Yeah." Trey's flat response didn't invite confidences. He hunkered down on his heels, cowboy-style, a blade of grass in the corner of his mouth, staring at the buildings of the Lazy H far below.

"Your dad was my best friend all through school," Lucas said, ignoring Trey's refusal to look at him. "We were as close as brothers—closer maybe than even Josh and I were. I always planned to rodeo when I got out of school, spent every minute I could practicing roping and riding. Rodeoing was Clay's dream, too, but he fell in love with your mom in high school. She was a pretty little thing and he was crazy about her, but she didn't like the amount of time he spent with me—I think she resented how close we were. Clay and I graduated from high school and went down the road, leaving your mom behind.

"She graduated the next year and started traveling with us, but she still didn't like me. She told me once that she hated coming second with Clay, that he always put his friendship with me first, over his love for her. I tried to tell her that she was wrong, but she wouldn't listen."

"Was she wrong?"

Lucas glanced sideways at the boy, who continued to stare down the slope of the butte.

"Yeah, she was wrong," he said, his voice firm with conviction. "If there's one thing I know is true, it's that Clay loved Suzie more than anything else on earth. I stood up with them as best man the day they got married—Clay was over the moon, he was so happy. Two months later, she was pregnant, and he thought he owned the world. Unfortunately, that's when the trouble started."

Lucas felt rather than saw the quick motion of Trey's head as he glanced at him before facing forward again. "Suzie loved to party, and Clay was worried about her carrying the baby. He wanted her to stay home and take better care of her health—she'd had a few minor problems early on, and he was scared to death that something would happen to her or you.''

"And instead, something happened to him." Trey's voice was still expressionless, but his body was tense as he listened.

"Yeah." Lucas nodded slowly. "Suzie was nearly six months pregnant with you when they had a hell of a fight. He wanted her to stay home on Saturday night—she wanted him to go with her to a party with friends. They had words and Clay insisted that she think of his baby first." Lucas paused. He couldn't bring himself to tell Trey that Suzie had raged, responding by lying and telling Clay that the baby she carried wasn't his. Nor that she'd purposely twisted the knife tighter when she spitefully told him that her child was fathered by Lucas.

The silence lasted so long that Trey glanced at Lucas, who was staring unseeingly at the Lazy H buildings below.

At last, Lucas's voice began again, rasping rustily. "Anyway, they fought. Clay had too much to drink and showed up at the barns where I was nursing a sick horse. He was spoiling for a fight. I tried to reason with him and kept ducking punches, but it didn't do any good. The horses were getting spooked and your mom walked into the barn looking for him just about the time he threw another punch. She screamed and ran into the stall, your dad yelled and the horse panicked. I got Suzie out of the stall, but your dad fell and the horse kicked him, clipped the back of his head with his metal horseshoe. He died instantly.''

Trey was crying silently. Tears welled and overflowed, dripping down his cheeks. He lifted a fist and rubbed them off his cheeks.

"So you didn't kill him. Why does my mom think you did?" His voice was thick, harsh with tears.

"If I'd listened to your mother, helped her talk Clay into leaving the rodeo and settling down with her in Butte Creek, our fight in the barn would never have happened and he'd be alive today," Lucas said grimly. "You were right, son, it should have been me that died that night, not Clay."

Trey stared straight ahead, visibly trying to control the seemingly never-ending well of tears.

"I never had a chance to know my dad, but I don't believe you killed him. Murphy told me that when it's your time, God takes you. Doesn't matter how old or how young you are, he calls and you go." He looked at Lucas, his eyes old beyond their years and clear with understanding. "I don't think it would have made any difference what you did, Lucas, it was my dad's time. Nothing you did could have changed that."

Lucas stared at him, unable to speak, only now realizing that buried deep in his wounded heart was the hope that Clay's son could forgive him for the loss of his father. Now Trey offered him forgiveness, openhanded and without reservation. He sucked in a breath, trying to stem the heavy thickness that clogged his throat and fogged his eyes.

"It's all right, Lucas," the boy said. He laid a consoling hand on Lucas's shoulder. "I used to cry a lot about Dad being gone when I was a little kid, but today's the first time I've cried over him in years."

Lucas looked into the serious, youthful face and saw Clay's warm understanding lurking in that blue gaze. "Damn, kid," he said, fighting back the tears. "I miss him."

Trey squeezed his shoulder. "Me, too."

They sat there, the boy with his hand on the big man's shoulder, until Lucas could breathe again and Trey no longer had to wipe away tears.

Lucas cleared his throat and stood, holding out a hand to the teenager. "You ready to go home?"

Trey grinned, a slightly wobbly grin, but a grin nonetheless, and grabbed Lucas's hand to let him pull him onto his feet. "Home. That sounds good."

Jennifer and Josh paced the floor, poured endless cups of coffee that they didn't drink, and waited for Lucas to return.

"Here they come!" Josh yelled through the screen door and Jennifer hurried out to the porch. They waited impatiently while Lucas and Trey stripped their saddles and bridles from their horses and turned them loose in the corral. Trey walked out of the corral, stood talking to Lucas for a few seconds, then left him to head for the bunkhouse.

"Well?" Jennifer burst out, unable to contain herself any longer when Lucas reached the foot of the porch. He took the steps in two long strides and grabbed her.

"You were right." He planted a quick, hard kiss on her mouth and looked over her shoulder at Josh. "He listened—and he's more like Clay than I ever dared hope."

Josh searched Lucas's eyes for a long moment before he relaxed, expelling a heavy sigh. "Thank God," he grunted. "It's about time. I think I'll take myself off to Colby's." He tugged his hat on and winked at

Jennifer. "Probably won't be back until very, very late."

Jennifer frowned at him, blushing bright pink, and he laughed, taking the steps to the front gate with swift strides.

"What do you suppose he meant by that?" she demanded.

"Probably exactly what you think he meant," Lucas said, grinning at the flush that colored her cheeks. He pulled open the screen door and tugged her inside. Then he swung her up in his arms.

"We need to talk," he said sternly, and began to climb the stairs.

"Absolutely," she agreed. "Where are you taking me?"

"Somewhere private." He nudged his bedroom door open and used his heel to kick it shut. He strode to the bed and let her feet slide to the floor, his hands closing over her upper arms to hold her in front of him. "Are we courting?"

Jennifer blinked, confused, before she slowly answered. "Uh, yes. I think we're courting."

"Good. Then I assume we both have honorable intentions."

"Yes." She stared at him, wondering exactly where this was leading.

"And that we'll get married as soon as Montana state law allows."

"Oh," she gasped. "Lucas, I—"

"Unless you're going to say you love me, don't bother talking," he growled, his face determined. "Because I damn sure love you and I don't believe for a minute that you'd crawl all over me like you did last night unless you loved me, too."

"I didn't crawl all over you," she began indignantly before the rest of his words sank in. "Oh, Lucas. You love me."

"Yeah, I'm crazy about you." His gaze ran lovingly over her flushed, starry-eyed features and his hands left her shoulders so he could thread his fingers through the silky red-gold curls at her temples. "And I don't care how many husbands and lovers your mother had, I'm going to be the last and only for you."

"How did you know I was worried about that?" she asked him, startled by his insight.

"Because I know you, Teacher, and what I don't know, we'll work out." His mouth curved in a smile just before his lips found hers and tasted salt. He jerked back, worried. "What's wrong?"

"Nothing's wrong." Her smile was misty. "I love you, Lucas."

"It's about damn time you told me," he muttered before his mouth closed over hers and he tumbled them over onto the bed.

A week later, Jennifer sat curled on Lucas's lap, watching Trey throw a Frisbee for Beastie to chase.

"Do you think he's really okay with his mom?" she asked, toying with the open collar of his shirt.

"I think he's doing better," Lucas replied, smoothing his palm over her bare arm.

"He said she told him that she doesn't hate you anymore," she said, watching Beastie race after Trey. "Do you think it was good for him to go see her at the treatment center?"

"Yes, I think it was good for him to see her. He asked her about Clay and she talked about him more clearly than she ever has before. I hope she gets well and stays sober. I think it's a good sign that she agreed to let Trey stay with us until she's better able to make a home for him."

The screen door squeaked open behind them. Josh stepped in front of them, a duffel bag in one hand, a denim jacket slung over his shoulder.

"Where are you off to?" Lucas asked.

"I'm leaving, Lucas," Josh said quietly. "Kenny Wilson offered me a job scouting rodeo stock for him and I accepted."

Jennifer slipped off Lucas's lap and stepped aside while Lucas rose from the chair.

Lucas was stunned. "I never knew you were interested in scouting rodeo stock."

Josh shrugged. "I need to get away from Butte Creek for a while, Lucas, there are too many memories here. Maybe a change of scenery and new work will help."

"Damn." Lucas's shoulders sagged. He had a new perspective and acceptance of Josh's pain because of his love for Jennifer. "You know your bed will always be waiting, whenever you're ready to come home."

"I know." Josh stuck out his hand. Lucas crushed it in his and threw an arm around him, hugging him fiercely for one brief moment before releasing him. "Don't worry, Lucas," he said, his keen gaze searching Lucas's face. "I won't be drinking anymore. You were right, it's time to get on with my life."

"Good," Lucas said gruffly. "It's nice to know I won't need to fight my way out of a saloon with you any time soon."

Josh grinned and turned to Jennifer. "Give me a hug, sister-to-be. I have to be in Miles City before tomorrow."

Jennifer gladly returned his hug.

"Take care of yourself," she whispered.

"I will. So long."

Lucas slipped an arm around her waist and they watched Josh climb into his pickup, wave goodbye, and leave, dust billowing up behind him down the lane.

"He'll be back, Lucas." She tipped her head back and looked up at him. "He just needs time."

His chest lifted in a deep sigh. "I know," he said, tucking her head under his chin and gazing off across the lawn at Trey, laughing as Beastie tackled him to get the Frisbee. "You know, honey," he said slowly, "I've been thinking—don't you think Beastie and Trey need another brother?"

Jennifer's gaze followed his and found the two just as Trey wrestled the red plastic disk away from the big dog. "You mean a puppy?"

"No, I was thinking more along the lines of a baby."

Jennifer's heart stopped. His hand caught her chin and tilted her face up to his.

"I think that's a wonderful idea. But don't you think we should get married first?"

"Oh, yeah. We'll do that tomorrow. In the meantime," he declared, swinging her up in his arms and opening the screen door, "I think we should practice making babies."

She smiled and kissed the underside of his jaw. "With luck, we'll have to practice a lot."

He laughed, the deep, throaty chuckle she loved, and carried her up the stairs.

*   *   *   *   *

COMING NEXT MONTH

#1039 MEGGIE'S BABY—Cheryl Reavis
That Special Woman!
Reuniting with her lost love, Jack Begaye, gave Meg Baron everything she dreamed of—a husband and a father for her unborn baby. But would their newfound happiness last when Meg's past threatened their future?

#1040 NO LESS THAN A LIFETIME—Christine Rimmer
The Jones Gang
Although Faith Jones had loved Price Montgomery from afar for years, she never dared dream that he'd return her feelings. Then a night of passion changed everything—and Faith wouldn't settle for anything less than a lifetime....

#1041 THE BACHELOR AND THE BABY WISH—
Kate Freiman
Hope Delacorte had one last chance to have the baby she so wanted, but there seemed to be no prospective fathers in sight...unless she turned to friend Josh Kincaid. He'd offered to father her child—no strings attached—but that was before they started to fall in love.

#1042 FULL-TIME FATHER—Susan Mallery
Erin Ridgeway had just given Parker Hamilton the biggest news of his life—he was the father of the five-year-old niece she had been raising. Suddenly, being a full-time father and husband started to sound very appealing to Parker....

#1043 A GOOD GROOM IS HARD TO FIND—Amy Frazier
Sweet Hope Weddings
Country doctor Rhune Sherman certainly met his match when Tess McQueen arrived in town. But she had a score to settle, and he didn't want to think about the raging attraction between them—until the good folks of Sweet Hope decided to do a little matchmaking!

#1044 THE ROAD BACK HOME—Sierra Rydell
When Billy Muktoyuk left home, he impulsively left behind his high school sweetheart, Siksik Toovak, the only woman he'd ever loved. Now he was back—and there wasn't anything that would stop him from winning back her heart.

Made in MONTANA

by Jackie Merritt

The Fanon family—born and raised in
Big Sky Country...and heading for a wedding!

Meet them in these books from
Silhouette Special Edition® and
Silhouette Desire® beginning with:

MONTANA FEVER
Desire #1014, July 1996

MONTANA PASSION
That Special Woman!
Special Edition #1051,September 1996

And look for more MADE IN MONTANA titles
in 1996 and 1997!

Don't miss these stories of ranching and love
only from Silhouette Books!

Silhouette®
™

Available in June from

SINGLE IN SEATTLE
by Carolyn Zane

A salesclerk in the men's suits department, Clare Banning, gets jilted by her fiancé for being too boring. So she places a personal ad in a suit jacket pocket, then waits for a hunk to buy it. If only her ex-groom-to-be could see just how *un*boringly she kisses her new groom-to-be!

THE GROOM WHO (ALMOST) GOT AWAY
by *New York Times* bestselling author
Carla Neggers

Calley Hastings eats bagels, has never seen a horse close up and doesn't know much about kids. Her ex, Max Slade, eats grits, runs a ranch and is raising his three orphaned little brothers—who decide it's high time to hoodwink Calley into coming home to Wyoming....

Love—when you least expect it!

This July, watch for the delivery of...

An exciting new miniseries that appears in a different Silhouette series each month. It's about love, marriage—and Daddy's unexpected need for a baby carriage!

Daddy Knows Last unites five of your favorite authors as they weave five connected stories about baby fever in New Hope, Texas.

- **THE BABY NOTION** by Dixie Browning
  (SD#1011, 7/96)

- **BABY IN A BASKET** by Helen R. Myers
  (SR#1169, 8/96)

- **MARRIED...WITH TWINS!**
  by Jennifer Mikels
  (SSE#1054, 9/96)

- **HOW TO HOOK A HUSBAND (AND A BABY)**
  by Carolyn Zane
  (YT#29, 10/96)

- **DISCOVERED: DADDY** by Marilyn Pappano
  (IM#746, 11/96)

Daddy Knows Last arrives in July...only from